Praise for

THE EIGHT MOUNTAINS

"A fine book, a rich, achingly painful story that is made for all of us who have ever felt a hunger for the mountains. Few books have so accurately described the way stony heights can define one's sense of joy and rightness. And it is an exquisite unfolding of the deep way humans may love one another."

—Annie Proulx

"*The Eight Mountains* is an old-fashioned novel in the best sense of the word. With gorgeously understated, unhurried prose, Cognetti crafts the story of an unlikely friendship between a city boy named Pietro and a young cow herder, Bruno, who lives in the Alpine mountains where the members of Pietro's family spend their vacations. . . . Cognetti's mix of patient observation and sharp insight into the natural world recalls the mastery of Helen Macdonald's *H Is for Hawk*. . . . Even though Pietro is solitary and remote, one can't help caring for him. The brilliant writing helps, but there's something more: His love for nature is profound, a sign that deep currents swirl beneath his crotchety surface, pulling the reader into the vortex of his emotions. Carnell and Segre capture the tone of Cognetti's calm descriptions of nature, setting them in tense contrast with Pietro's discordant thoughts."

—*The New York Times Book Review*

"Cognetti's novel elegantly paints the terrifyingly beautiful landscape of the mountains at the heart of a brotherly friendship that proves to transcend anything."

—*Booklist*

"A slim novel of startling expansion that subtly echoes its setting."

—V

"A moving meditation on man in time and natur"

"Could Cognetti be the new Elena Ferrante

wer

"A novel that deals with deep themes—friendship, the relationship between generations, the management of one's life—in simple and precise yet evocative language."

—*Corriere della Sera*

"A timeless novel."

—*Panorama*

"Through essential yet extraordinarily evocative and intense language, Cognetti constructs a short novel that many have already called a classic, in which one can undoubtedly hear the echo of the masters who inspired it."

—*Critica Letteraria*

"*The Eight Mountains* is written in such arrestingly simple language—you can almost feel the Italian phrasing in the translation from Simon Carnell and Erica Segre—that it's impossible not to be gradually sucked into the peaks and valleys of Pietro's life. . . . [T]here's something about the vertiginous setting that lends itself to this kind of contemplation. Cognetti captures the elation and melancholy that comes with reaching a spectacular summit, only to realize the minuscule part we play in the panorama of life."

—*The Guardian*

"There is something of [Cognetti's] countryman Primo Levi in the wonderfully lucid sentences and contemplative tone of his prose. . . . A beautifully crafted piece of writing, whose inevitable conclusion movingly sees the past repeat itself."

—*The Irish Times*

"*The Eight Mountains* is a novel about love for the mountains, but more than that it is about those male relationships that rely on the slow accumulation of understanding where nothing is directly expressed: men, while feeling a lot, say very little, and tragically, sometimes this can be fatal. Cognetti's novel, poetic and properly romantic, achieves a moving grandeur."

—*The Sunday Times* (UK)

THE EIGHT MOUNTAINS

A Novel

PAOLO COGNETTI

Translated by Simon Carnell and Erica Segre

WASHINGTON SQUARE PRESS

ATRIA

New York • London • Toronto • Sydney • New Delhi

An Imprint of Simon & Schuster, Inc.
1230 Avenue of the Americas
New York, NY 10020

This book is a work of fiction. Any references to historical events, real people, or real places are used fictitiously. Other names, characters, places, and events are products of the author's imagination, and any resemblance to actual events or places or persons, living or dead, is entirely coincidental.

Originally published in Italy in 2016 by Giulio Einaudi editore s.p.a. Turin, under the title *Le otto montagne*
Published by agreement with MalaTesta Literary Agency, Milan

First Washington Square Press/Atria Paperback edition February 2019

WASHINGTON SQUARE PRESS/**ATRIA** PAPERBACK and colophon are trademarks of Simon & Schuster, Inc.

Interior design by Dana Sloan

Manufactured in the United States of America

10 9 8 7 6 5 4 3 2 1

Library of Congress Cataloging-in-Publication Data

Names: Cognetti, Paolo, 1978– author. | Carnell, Simon, 1962– translator. | Segre, Erica, translator.
Title: The eight mountains : a novel / Paolo Cognetti ; translated by Simon Carnell and Erica Segre.
Other titles: Otto montagne. English
Description: First Atria Books hardcover edition. | New York : Atria Books, March 2018.
Identifiers: LCCN 2017038835 (print) | LCCN 2017048427 (ebook) | ISBN 9781501169908 (ebook) | ISBN 9781501169885 (hardback) | ISBN 9781501169892 (paperback)
Subjects: | BISAC: FICTION / Literary. | FICTION / Coming of Age. | FICTION / General.
Classification: LCC PQ4903.O36 (ebook) | LCC PQ4903.O36 O8813 2018 (print) | DDC 853/.92—dc23
LC record available at https://lccn.loc.gov/2017038835

ISBN 978-1-5011-6988-5
ISBN 978-1-5011-6989-2 (pbk)
ISBN 978-1-5011-6990-8 (ebook)

FONTANE 2014–2016

This story is for the friend who inspired it,
guiding me where there is no path.
And for the Faith and Luck that protected it from the start,
with all my love.

Farewell! Farewell! But this I tell
To thee, thou Wedding-Guest!
He prayeth well, who loveth well
Both man and bird and beast.

—SAMUEL TAYLOR COLERIDGE,
"THE RIME OF THE ANCIENT MARINER"

PROLOGUE

MY FATHER HAD his own way of going to the mountains: scarcely inclined to meditation, full of obstinacy and arrogance. He would climb headlong, without pacing himself, always competing with someone or something, and where the trail seemed overlong he would take a short cut via the steepest slope. When you were with him it was forbidden to stop—complaining about hunger or the cold was not permitted—but you were allowed to sing a good song, especially when caught in a storm or in thick fog. And to whoop whilst flinging yourself down a snowfield.

My mother, who had known him since he was a boy, used to say that even then he would wait for nobody, intent as he was on pursuing anyone glimpsed up ahead: it was only a strong pair of legs that could make you desirable in his eyes, and she hinted, laughing, that this was how she had seduced him. Later on, once the uphill race had begun, she preferred to sit in a meadow, or to soak her feet in a stream, or to identify by name the herbs and flowers. At the summit she liked more than anything to gaze at the distant peaks, to reflect on those of her youth, and to remember when she had reached them and with whom—while my father at that point was overcome by a kind of disappointment, and just wanted to return home.

I think that these were completely opposite reactions to the same shared sense of nostalgia. My parents had migrated to the city in their early thirties, leaving behind the Veneto countryside where my mother had been born, and where my father had been raised as an orphan of the war. Their first mountains, their first love, had been the Dolomites. They would sometimes name them in their conversations, when I was still too young to follow what they were saying but could sense how certain words rang out: special sounds that were charged with additional meaning. The Catinaccio, Sassolungo, Tofane, and the Marmolada. All it took was for my father to utter one of these words, and my mother's eyes would light up.

These were the places where they had fallen in love, as even I came to understand after a while: it had been a priest who had taken them there as adolescents, and it was the very same priest who had married them, one autumn morning, in front of the little chapel found at the foot of the Tre Cime di Lavaredo. This marriage in the mountains was the foundational myth of our family. Boycotted by my mother's parents, for reasons unknown to me; celebrated with a handful of friends, in anoraks instead of wedding attire, and with a bed in the Auronzo refuge for their first night as husband and wife. The snow was already sparkling on the ledges of Cima Grande. It was a Saturday in October in 1972, the end of the climbing season for that year and for many years to come. The next day they packed their leather climbing boots and plus fours into the car, together with her pregnancy and the contract for his new job, and headed for Milan.

• • •

Calmness was not a virtue my father set much store by, but in the city it was more necessary than the lungs needed for climbing. In the seventies in Milan we lived in an apartment building with a panoramic view, above a broad avenue of traffic beneath the asphalt of which, it was said, the Olona river ran. And although it is true that on rainy days the road would become flooded—and I would imagine the subterranean river roaring beneath it in the dark, so swollen as to burst from the drains—it was that other river coursing with cars, vans, scooters, lorries, buses, and ambulances which seemed always to be in full spate. We lived high up, on the seventh floor, and the two ranks of identical buildings that lined the road amplified the noise. Some nights my father could stand it no longer; he would get out of bed and fling open the window as if he wanted to inveigh against the city, to compel it to be quiet, or to douse it with boiling pitch. He would stand there for a moment looking down, then slip on his coat and go out to walk around.

Through those windowpanes we could see a lot of sky. Uniformly white, oblivious to the changing seasons, marked only by the flight of birds. My mother obstinately persisted in cultivating flowers on the small balcony that was blackened by exhaust fumes and mold-stained by the rain. On that balcony, whilst tending her fragile plants, she would tell me about vineyards in August, about the countryside in which she had grown up, about the tobacco leaves hung from the racks in the drying kiln, or about the asparagus that, if it were to remain tender and white, had to be cut before it pierced the soil's surface—requiring a rare talent to spot it whilst still underground.

Now that sharp eye of hers had become useful in a radically different context. In the Veneto she had been a nurse, but once in Milan she secured a position as a health worker in the "Elms" district in the western outskirts of the city, in a working-class neighborhood. It was a role that had just been created, together with the equally new family clinic in which she worked providing support for women during pregnancy and following the development of the newborn infants in their first year of life. This was my mother's work, and she liked it. The only thing was that the area where she had been sent to carry it out made it seem more like a mission. Actual elms in these parts were few and far between: the entire toponymy of the neighborhood, with its streets named after alders, spruce, larches, and birch trees, contrasted mockingly with the twelve-story, barracklike housing blocks infested with social ills of every kind. Among my mother's duties was the evaluation of the conditions in which a child was being raised, on visits that affected her deeply for days afterwards. In the most serious cases she was obliged to refer children to the juvenile court. It cost her a great deal of anguish to reach such a point, in addition to receiving a dose of insults and threats, and yet despite this she never doubted that she had reached the right decision. She was not alone in this conviction: the social workers, the educationalists, the schoolteachers were united by a deep-seated solidarity, a feminine sense of collective responsibility towards these children.

My father on the other hand had always been a loner. He worked as a chemist in a factory—with a ten-thousand-strong workforce, constantly subject to strike action and sackings—and whatever had taken place in there, he would return home in the evening full of anger. At suppertime he would stare in silence at the TV news, gripping his cutlery in midair, as if he expected at any moment the outbreak of another world war; and he would curse to himself at the news of every murder victim, every governmental crisis, every hike in the price of oil, every bombing by unidentified terrorists. With the few colleagues he would invite home he discussed almost exclusively political issues, and always ended up in an argument. He would cast himself as anticommunist with communists, as a radical with Catholics, as a freethinker with anyone who presumed to confine him in a church or on a list of party members. But these were not times during which you could escape all allegiance, and after a while my father's workmates stopped coming round. Yet he continued to go to work as if he were climbing every morning into the trenches. He continued not to sleep at night, to take things too much to heart, to wear earplugs and take pills for his headaches, to explode in violent fits of rage—at which point my mother would spring into action, since along with her marital duties she had also assumed the role of pacifying him, of muffling the blows in the fight between my father and the world.

• • •

At home they still spoke the dialect of the Veneto. To my ears it sounded like a secret language that they shared, the echo of a mysterious previous life. A remnant of the past, just like the three photographs my mother had displayed on a small table in the entrance hall. I would often stop to look at them. The first was a portrait of her parents in Venice, during the only trip they had ever taken, a gift from my grandfather to my grandmother to celebrate their silver wedding anniversary. In the second her entire family had posed for the camera during the grape harvest: my grandparents sat at the center of the group, three girls and a young man standing around them, the baskets filled with grapes in the courtyard of the barn. In the third my grandparents' only male offspring, my uncle, smiled together with my father next to a summit cross, dressed in mountaineering gear and with a rope wound round his shoulder. My uncle had died young, and that was why I bore his name, though I was called Pietro and he was Piero, in our family lexicon. And yet of all these people I had known none. I was never taken to visit them, nor did they ever turn up for a visit in Milan. A few times a year my mother would take a train of a Saturday morning, and come back Sunday evening a little sadder than she'd left. Then she would get over it and life would continue. There was too much to be done, and too many people to care for, to indulge in melancholy.

But that past had a way of leaping out at you when you least expected it. Long car journeys were necessary to take me to school, my mother to the clinic, and my father to the factory, and on certain mornings she would sing an old song. She would begin the first verse in the traffic, and soon after we would join in. These songs were set in the mountains during the Great War: "The Troop Train," "The Sugana Valley," "The Captain's Testament." They told stories that I, too, now knew by heart: twenty-seven had departed for the front, and only five had returned. Down there on the battlefield of the Piave stood a cross for a mother who would sooner or later come in search of it. Far away a betrothed waited, sighing, then tired of waiting and married another—the dying man would send her a kiss, and ask for a flower in return. I understood from the words of dialect in these songs that my parents had carried them from their previous life, but I also sensed something different and strange—that is to say that these songs also spoke directly about the two of them, who knows how. I mean about the two of them specifically: how else to explain the degree of emotion that their voices so clearly betrayed?

Then on certain rare windy days, in autumn or spring, at the end of Milanese streets, the mountains would appear. It would happen after a bend in the road, above an overpass, suddenly, and the gaze of both my parents would immediately switch there, without one needing to point out anything to the other. The peaks were white, the sky a rare blue, the sensation as of a miracle. Down below, where we lived, were factories in turmoil, overcrowded social housing, riots in the piazza, abused children, teenage mothers: up there, the snow. My mother would ask then which mountains were in view, and my father would look around as if navigating the urban geography with a compass. Which avenue is this: Monza, Zara? Then it must be La Grigna, he would say, having thought about it a bit. Yes, I'm sure that it is really her. I remembered the story well: La Grigna was a most beautiful and cruel warrior who had killed with her arrows the knights who climbed to declare their love for her—so God had punished her by turning her into a mountain. And now she was there, through the windscreen, allowing herself to be admired by the three of us, each one with a different, silent thought. Then the lights changed, a pedestrian would run across, someone sounded the horn, my father would tell them where to get off and change gear furiously, accelerating away from that moment of grace.

• • •

The end of the seventies arrived, and while Milan was burning the two of them put on their climbing boots again. They did not head east, from where they had come, but west, as if continuing their flight, towards the Ossola, the Valsesia, the Val d'Aosta; towards mountains that were still higher and more severe. My mother would later tell me that at first she had been overcome by an unexpected feeling of oppression. Compared to the gentle contours of the Veneto and the Trentino these western valleys seemed narrow, dark, enclosed like gorges; the rock was damp and black, streams and waterfalls plunging down from everywhere. So much water, she thought. It must rain a lot here. She had not realized that all of that water originated in an exceptional source, nor that she and my father were heading straight for it. They climbed up one of the valleys until they were high enough to emerge again into sunlight: from there the landscape suddenly opened up, and before their eyes stood Monte Rosa. An Arctic world, a permanent winter, looming over the summer pastures. It frightened my mother. But my father would say that for him it had been like discovering a new scale of grandeur: like arriving from the mountains of men to find yourself in the mountains of giants. And naturally he fell in love with them at first sight.

I don't know exactly where they were on that day. Whether it was Macugnaga, Alagna, Gressoney, Ayas. At that time we would holiday in a different place each year, following my father on his restless wandering all around the mountain that had conquered him. Better than the valleys I remember the houses in which we stayed, if you could call them houses: we would rent a bungalow in a campsite, or a room in a hostel, and stay there for a couple of weeks. There was never enough room to make these places homely, or time enough to become attached to anything, but my father did not care for or even notice such things.

As soon as we arrived he would get changed—take from his bag the checked shirt, the corduroy trousers, the woolen jumper—and, wearing these old clothes again, he became a different man. He would spend the short vacation exploring the mountain paths, leaving early in the morning and returning in the evening, or even the next day—covered in dust, burnt by the sun, tired and happy. Over supper he would talk of the chamois and the Alpine ibexes, of nights spent bivouacked, of starlit skies, of snow that at such altitude fell even in August, and when he was most happy he would end by saying: I really wish that you could have been there with me.

The fact of the matter is that my mother refused to climb the glacier. She harbored an irrational and unshakable fear of it: she used to say that, as far as she was concerned, the mountain ended at three thousand meters, the altitude, that is, of her own range, the Dolomites. She preferred two thousand meters to three—the meadows, rivers, woods—and deeply loved one thousand too, the life there of those villages of wood and stone. When my father was away she liked to go for walks with me, to drink a coffee in the square, to sit in a meadow and read to me from a book, to exchange a few words with a passerby. She reluctantly endured our constant changes of place. She often pleaded with my father that she would prefer a house that she could make her own, and a village to return to, and he would tell her that there wasn't enough money for another rent, in addition to that of the apartment in Milan. But she managed to negotiate with him a budget that was within their means, and finally he allowed her to begin searching for a place of our own.

In the evenings, as soon as the remains of supper had been cleared away, my father would unfold a map onto the table and begin planning the next day's route. He had beside him the gray booklet of the Italian Alpine Club and a half-filled glass of grappa that he would occasionally sip from. My mother would take advantage of her own moment of freedom by sitting in an armchair or on the bed and immersing herself in a novel: for an hour or two she would disappear into its pages, as if she were elsewhere. It was then that I would climb onto my father's lap to see what he was up to. I would find him to be cheerful and talkative, the complete opposite of the father I was used to in the city. He was happy to show me the map and how to read it. This is a glacial stream, he would point out to me, this is a lake, and this is a group of mountain huts. Here you can distinguish the forest by its color, the alpine meadow, the scree, the glacier. These curved lines indicate the altitude: the closer together they are, the steeper the mountain, up to the point where it is impossible to climb further; and here where the lines are further apart the incline is gentler and the paths follow it, can you see? These triangles accompanied by a figure for the altitude represent the summits. And it's to the summits that we're going. We only start descending when it's impossible to climb higher. Understand?

No, I could not understand. I needed to see it, this world that filled him with such joy. Years later, when we started to go there together, my father claimed to recall the precise moment at which my vocation manifested itself. One morning as my mother still slept and he was preparing to leave, he looked up from lacing his boots to see me standing there, already fully dressed and ready to follow him. I must have dressed myself whilst still in bed. I had startled him in the darkness, looking much older than my six or seven years. According to his version of the event I was already what I would become later: it was a premonition of his adult son, a ghost of the future.

"Don't you want to sleep a little longer?" he asked, speaking softly so as not to wake my mother.

"I want to come with you," I'd replied, or so he would claim. But perhaps it was just the phrase that he liked to remember.

ONE

The Mountain of Childhood

ONE

THE VILLAGE OF GRANA was located on the periphery of one of those valleys ignored as irrelevant by those who passed by it, sealed in as it was by iron-gray peaks above, and by a cliff that obstructed access from below. On the top of the cliff the ruins of a tower still looked out across overgrown fields. A dirt track deviated from the regional trunk road and climbed steeply, in circles, up to the foot of the tower; then, getting less steep beyond it, the track turned up the flank of the mountain and entered the great valley at its midpoint before continuing on a slight slope. It was in July of 1984 that we first took it. They were scything hay in the fields. The valley proved to be more extensive than it appeared from below, covered by forest on the side that was in shadow, and terraced on the side that was in sunlight; down below, amongst the thickets of bushes, ran a river that I glimpsed intermittently, sparkling—and this was the first thing about Grana that appealed to me. I was reading adventure stories at the time, and it was Mark Twain who had induced in me a love of rivers. I thought that down there you could fish, dive, swim, cut down some small tree and build a raft, and absorbed in such fantasies I hardly noticed the village that had come into view after a curve in the road.

"This is it," my mother said. "Go slowly."

My father slowed to a walking pace. Since starting out he had followed her directions obediently. He lowered his head, looking right and left through the dust raised by the car, his gaze dwelling on the stables, the chicken coops, the log-built haylofts, the charred or collapsed dwellings, the tractors at the edge of the road, the hay balers. Two black dogs wearing bells around their necks sprang out from a courtyard. Apart from a couple of newer houses, the whole village seemed to be made of the same gray rock as the mountain and clung to it like an outcrop, or an ancient landslide. A little further up, goats were grazing.

My father said nothing. My mother, who had discovered this place on her own, pointed out where to park and got out of the car to look for the owner while we unloaded the luggage. One of the dogs came towards us, barking, and my father did something I'd never seen him do before: he stretched out a hand for it to sniff, spoke to it gently, and stroked it between its ears. Perhaps he got on better with dogs than with his own kind.

"And so?" he asked me, as we unhooked the elastics from the roof rack. "What do you think of it?"

It's beautiful, I would like to have answered. A smell of hay, stable, wood, smoke, and who knows what else had enveloped me as soon as I'd stepped out of the car, full of promise. But unsure as to whether this was the right answer or not, I had replied instead: "It's not bad. What do you think?"

My father shrugged his shoulders. He looked up over the suitcases and glanced at the shack that stood before us. It was leaning to one side, and would surely have collapsed if it weren't for the two poles that were propping it up. Inside, it was crammed with bales of hay, and above the hay there was a denim shirt that someone had taken off there and forgotten.

"I grew up in a place like this," he said, without letting me know whether this was a good or a bad thing.

He grabbed the handle of a suitcase and was about to take it down when something else occurred to him. He looked at me, thinking of something that evidently caused him great amusement.

"In your opinion, can the past happen again?"

"It's difficult," I said, so as not to be wrong-footed. He was always asking me riddles of this kind. He saw in me an intelligence similar to his own, inclined towards logic and mathematics, and thought that it was his duty to exercise it.

"Look at that river," he said. "Can you see it? Let's suppose that the water is time passing. If where we are now is the present, where do you think the future is located?"

I thought about it for a moment. It seemed like an easy one. I gave the most obvious answer: "The future is where the water goes, down over there."

"Wrong!" my father declared. "Fortunately."

Then, as if he had freed himself from a great burden, he said "*Oopala,*" the word he used to use when picking something up, including me, and the first of the two suitcases fell to the ground with a thud.

The house my mother had rented was in the upper part of the village, in a courtyard set around a drinking trough. It bore the signs of two distinct periods. The first was that of its walls, balconies of blackened larch, a roof of moss-covered slates, the large soot-stained chimney, all pointing to its venerable origins. The second was merely dated: a period in which, inside the house, layers of linoleum had been used to cover the floor, floral wallpaper had been hung, fitted cabinets and the basin had been installed in the kitchen, all now damp-stained and faded. The only object that could be salvaged from this mediocrity was a black stove, made of cast iron, massive and severe, with a brass handle and four hotplates on which to cook. It must have been reclaimed from another place and time altogether. I think that what my mother liked more than anything else was what was not actually there, because she had found in effect a house that was more or less empty. She asked the proprietress if we could improve it a bit, and she had simply replied: "Do what you like." She had not rented it out for years, and in all likelihood had not expected to do so that summer. She was brusque in her manner but not impolite. I think she was embarrassed, since she had come from working in the fields and had not had time to change. She handed to my mother a large iron key, finished saying something about the hot water, and gave a brief show of resistance before accepting the envelope that my mother had prepared.

By this time my father had made himself scarce. For him one house was much like another, and the next day he was expected back in the office. He had gone out onto the balcony for a smoke, his hands on the coarse wood of the balustrade, his eyes scrutinizing the summits. It looked as if he were surveying them in order to calculate from which angle to launch an assault. He came back in after the owner of the house had left, so as to be spared any pleasantries, in a somber mood that had come upon him in the meantime. He said that he was going out to get something for lunch, and that he wanted to be back in the car before the evening.

• • •

In that house, once my father had gone, my mother reverted to a version of herself that I had never known before. In the morning, as soon as she had got out of bed she would put some kindling in the stove, scrunch up a page of newspaper, and strike a match on the rough surface of the cast iron. She wasn't bothered by the smoke that would then unfurl into the kitchen, or by the need to wrap ourselves in a blanket until the room warmed up, or by the milk that she would overheat and burn on the scalding hotplate. For breakfast she would give me toast and jam. She would wash me under the tap, scrubbing my face, neck, and ears before drying me with a kitchen rag and sending me on my way outdoors: out into the wind and the rain, so that I would finally lose a little of my delicate urban constitution.

On those days I would set about exploring the river. There were two boundaries that I was not allowed to cross: upstream a small wooden bridge beyond which the banks steepened increasingly and narrowed into a gully, downstream the thickets at the foot of the cliff where the water followed its course to the valley floor. This was the territory that my mother could control from the balcony of the house, but for me it was as good as having the whole river itself. That river coursed down crags at first, falling in a series of foaming rapids between huge rocks which I peered over to observe the silver reflections at the bottom. Further on it slowed and meandered, as if transformed from youth to adulthood, and cut around islets, colonized by birch trees, that I could leap across to reach the opposite bank. Further on still, a tangle of timber formed a barrier. At this point a gorge descended, and it had been an avalanche during winter that had torn down the trunks and branches that were now rotting in the water, though at the time I knew nothing of such things. In my eyes it was the moment in the life of the river when it simply encountered an obstacle, then stopped and stagnated. I would always end up sitting there, watching the weed that was undulating just below the surface of the water.

There was a young boy who grazed cows in the meadows along the banks of the river. According to my mother he was the nephew of the woman who owned the house. He always carried with him a yellow stick, made of plastic and with a curved handle, with which he would prod the cows towards the tall grass. There were seven of them, all chestnut-colored and restless. The boy would scold them when they wandered off by themselves, and would occasionally chase after one or another of them, cursing; while on the way back he would climb the slope and turn to call out to them with an *Oh, oh, oh*, or an *Eh, eh, eh* until, reluctantly, they would follow him to the stable. In the pasture he would sit down and watch them from above, carving a small piece of wood with his penknife.

"You can't stay there," he said, the one time that he spoke to me.

"Why not?" I asked.

"You're trampling the grass."

"So where can I stay?"

"Over there."

He pointed to the other side of the river. I could not see how to reach it from where I was standing, but I did not want to ask him or to negotiate a passage through his grass. So I stepped into the water without taking off my shoes. I tried to keep upright in the current and to show no hesitation, as if fording rivers was an everyday occurrence for me. I managed to cross, sat down with my trousers soaked and my shoes streaming, but when I turned to look at the boy he was no longer paying any attention to me.

We spent a good few days in this way, on opposite banks of the river, not deigning to notice each other.

"Why don't you try to make friends with him?" my mother asked, one evening in front of the stove. The house was impregnated with the damp of too many winters, so we would light the fire during supper and stay up warming ourselves until it was time for bed. We would both be reading our books, and every so often, between one page and another, the fire and our conversation were rekindled. The great black stove was listening to us.

"But how can I?" I answered. "I don't know what to say."

"You just say hello. Ask him what he's called. Ask him what his cows are called."

"OK, good night," I said, pretending to be absorbed in my reading.

When it came to social interaction my mother was well ahead of me. Since there were no shops in the village, while I was exploring my river she discovered the stable where you could buy milk and cheese, the allotment that sold certain types of vegetables, and the sawmill for a supply of offcuts of wood. She had also come to an arrangement with the young man from the dairy, who every morning and evening passed by in his van to collect the milk churns, so that he would deliver to us bread and a few groceries. And I'm not sure how she did it, but by our second week she had hung flower baskets on the balcony and filled them with geraniums. Now our house could be recognized from a distance, and she was already hearing the sparse inhabitants of Grana greeting her by her name.

"Anyway, it doesn't matter," I said, a minute later.

"What doesn't matter?"

"Making friends. I also like to be on my own."

"Oh, really?" my mother said. She raised her eyes from the page, and without smiling, as if it was a very serious matter, she added: "Are you sure about that?"

And with that she decided to help me herself. Not everyone is of the same opinion, but my mother was firmly convinced of the necessity to intervene in the lives of others. A couple of days later, in that same kitchen, I found the cow boy sitting on my own chair having breakfast. I smelt him, in fact, before seeing him, because he exuded the same smell of the stable, of hay, curdled milk, damp earth, and wood smoke which has always been for me, from that moment onwards, the smell of the mountains—the smell that I have found in all mountains, anywhere in the world. His name was Bruno Guglielmina. Everyone in Grana had the same surname, he insisted on explaining, but the name Bruno was unique to him. He was just a few months older than me, born in November of '72. He devoured the biscuits that my mother offered him, as if he'd never eaten biscuits in his life before. The final discovery I made was that it wasn't just me studying him down in the pasture, while both of us pretended to be oblivious to each other. He had been studying me too.

"You like the river, don't you?" he asked.

"Yes."

"Can you swim?"

"A bit."

"Fish?"

"Not really."

"Come on, I'll show you something."

Saying this he jumped from the chair. I exchanged looks with my mother, then ran after him without a second thought.

Bruno took me to a place that I already knew, where the river passes through the shadow cast by the little wooden bridge. Speaking low when we had reached the riverbank he ordered me to remain as quiet and hidden as possible. Then he gradually raised himself above the rock he was crouching behind, until he was just able to peer over it. He signaled with his hand for me to wait. While I waited I looked at him: he had straw-blond hair and his neck was burnt by the sun. He wore trousers in a size not his own, rolled up at the ankles and low-slung, a caricature of a grown man. He also had the demeanor of an adult, a kind of seriousness in his voice and gestures: with a nod he commanded me to join him, and I obeyed. I peered over the rock to see what he was looking at. I did not know what I was supposed to see there: beyond the rock the river formed a small waterfall and a shadowy pool, probably knee-deep. The surface of the water was unsettled, agitated by the churning fall. At the edges floated a finger's depth of foam, and a large trapped branch sticking out diagonally had collected grass and sodden leaves around itself. It wasn't much of a spectacle, only water that had run there from the mountain. And yet it was spellbinding; I don't know why.

After staring hard at the pool for a while I saw the surface break slightly and realized that there was something moving beneath it. One, two, three, and then four tapering shadows with their snouts facing into the current, with only their tails moving slowly from side to side. Occasionally one of the shadows would shift suddenly before stopping in another place; at other times it would break the surface with its back before sinking below again—but always stayed pointing in the direction of the little waterfall. We were further down the valley than they were, which was why they had not noticed us yet.

"Are they trout?" I whispered.

"Fish," said Bruno.

"Do they always stay here?"

"Not always. Sometimes they change hole."

"But what are they doing?"

"Hunting," he replied, as if to him it was the most obvious thing. I, on the other hand, was learning about it for the first time. I had always thought that fish swam with the current, which seemed easiest, and not that they would use up their energy by going against it. The trout moved their tails just enough to remain stationary. I would like to have known what they were hunting. Perhaps it was the gnats that I could see skimming the surface before stopping as if trapped by it. I observed the scene carefully for a while, trying to understand it better, before Bruno suddenly lost interest and leapt to his feet, waving his arms so that the trout sped away in an instant. I went to have a look. They had fled from the center of the pool in every direction. I looked into the pool and all that I could see was the white and blue gravel at the bottom—and then I had to abandon it to follow Bruno as he rushed up the opposite bank of the river.

A little further on a solitary building loomed above the bank like the house of a watchman. It was falling to ruin amongst the nettles, the brambles, the wasps' nests desiccating in the sun. In this countryside there were so many ruins just like this one. Bruno placed his hands on the walls, at a point where they met in a corner that was all cracks, pulled himself up, and with two quick movements reached the first-floor window.

"Come on!" he said, peering out from above. But then neglected to wait for me. Perhaps to him there seemed no difficulty in my following, and it did not occur to him that I might need help. Or perhaps he was just accustomed to this: that whether easy or difficult, it was every man for himself. I copied him as best as I could. I scraped my arms on the sill of the small window, looked inside, and saw Bruno lowering himself through the trapdoor of the attic on a ladder that led to the lower room. I think I had already decided that I would follow him anywhere.

Down below in the semi-darkness there was a space subdivided by low walls into four rooms of equal size, resembling tanks. In the air hung a stagnant smell of mold and rotten wood. As my eyes gradually adjusted to the dark I saw that the floor was littered with cans, bottles, old newspapers, shirts in rags, four wrecked shoes, bits of rusty equipment. Bruno had bent down next to a large white polished stone in the shape of a wheel that was placed in a corner of one room.

"What is it?" I asked.

"The grindstone," he said. Then added: "The stone of the mill."

I bent down next to him to look. I knew what a grindstone was, but had never seen one with my own eyes before. I stretched out my hand. The stone was cold, slimy, and in the hole at its center moss that adhered to your fingertips like green mud had gathered. I felt my arms smarting with the scratches from the window ledge.

"We need to stand it up," Bruno said.

"Why?"

"So that it can roll."

"But where to?"

"What do you mean where to? Down, no?"

I shook my head, because I did not understand. Bruno explained, patiently: "We stand it upright. We push it outside. And then we roll it down into the river. Then the fish will leap out of the river and we can eat them."

The idea seemed both awesome and impossible. That boulder-like weight was too much for us. But it was so lovely to imagine it rolling down, and to imagine that the two of us were capable of such a feat, that I decided to offer no objection. Someone must have already tried to move it, since between the stone and the floor two woodcutter's wedges had been inserted. They had gone under it just enough to raise it from the ground. Bruno picked up a stout stick, the handle of a pickaxe or a spade, and with a stone began to hammer it into that gap like a nail. When the end of it had wedged in, he worked the handle beneath the stone and stopped it with his foot.

"Now help me," he said.

"What should I do?"

I moved next to him. We were supposed to both push downwards, using the combined weight of our bodies to raise the millstone. So we clung together on the handle, and when my feet left the ground I felt, for a moment, that the great stone moved. Bruno had devised the right method, and with a better lever it might have worked, but that piece of old wood bent under our weight, creaking before eventually snapping in two and flinging us to the ground. One of his hands was injured. He let out a resounding curse.

"Have you hurt yourself?" I asked.

"Shitty stone," he said, sucking his wound. "Sooner or later, I'll move you from there." He climbed up the stepladder and disappeared above, moving furiously, and moments later I heard him jump down from the window and run away.

That evening I struggled to get to sleep. It was excitement that kept me awake: mine was a solitary childhood, and I wasn't used to doing things with others. In this respect too, I believed, I was just like my father. But that day I had felt something, an unexpected sense of intimacy that both attracted and frightened me, like an opening into unknown territory. To calm myself I sought for a mental image. I thought of the river: of the pool, of the small waterfall, of the trout that moved their tails to remain stationary, of the leaves and twigs that flowed elsewhere. And then of the trout darting to meet their prey. I began to understand a fact, namely that all things, for a river fish, come from upstream: insects, branches, leaves, everything. That's why it looks upstream, waiting for things to come. If the point at which you immerse yourself in the river is the present, I thought, then the past is the water that has flowed past you, that which has gone downstream and where there is nothing left for you; whereas the future is the water that comes down from above, bringing dangers and surprises. The past is in the valley, the future in the mountains. This is how I should have replied to my father. Whatever destiny may be, it resides in the mountains that tower over us.

Then gradually these thoughts also dispersed, and I lay awake listening. I was used by now to the sounds of the night, and could recognize them one after another. This, I thought, is the water flowing into the drinking trough. This is the bell on the collar of a dog on its nocturnal wanderings. This is the buzzing of Grana's solitary electric street lamp. I wondered whether Bruno in his own bed would be listening to the same sounds. My mother turned a page in the kitchen, while the crackle of the stove lulled me to sleep.

• • •

For the rest of that July not a day passed without us meeting up. Either I joined him in the pasture or Bruno strung a wire around his cows, connected it to a car battery, and turned up in our kitchen. More than the biscuits I think that it was my mother that he liked. He liked the attention she paid to him. She would question him openly, without preliminaries, as she was used to doing in her work, and he would answer, proud of the fact that his own story could be of interest to such a nice lady from the city. He told us that he was the youngest inhabitant of Grana, as well as the last boy left in the village, given that there was no prospect of any others. His father was away for the best part of the year, would turn up rarely and only in winter; and as soon as he sensed the arrival of spring in the air he would set off again for France or Switzerland, or wherever he could find a building site in need of workers. By contrast his mother had never moved from the village: in the fields above the houses she had a vegetable garden, a henhouse, two goats, beehives; her sole interest was in watching over this little kingdom. When he described her I recognized immediately who she was. A woman I had frequently seen passing me by, pushing a wheelbarrow or carrying a hoe and a rake; she would overtake me with her head down, seemingly oblivious to my existence. She lived with Bruno at an uncle's house; he was the husband of our landlady and the owner of some pastures and dairy cows. This uncle was in the mountains with his older cousins: Bruno gestured towards the window, through which at that moment I could only see woods and scree, and added that he would join them up there in August with the younger cows that had been left down below.

"In the mountains?" I asked.

"I mean in the mountain pastures. Do you know what an *alpeggio* is?"

I shook my head.

"And are your uncle and aunt nice to you?" my mother interrupted.

"Of course," said Bruno. "They have a lot to do."

"You do go to school though?"

"Oh sure."

"Do you like it?"

Bruno shrugged. He couldn't bring himself to say yes, even just to please her.

"And do your mother and father love each other?"

At this he looked away. He curled his lip into a grimace which might have meant no, or perhaps just a little, or that this was not a subject to stay there chatting about. The reply was enough to stop my mother from insisting further, since she had understood that there was something about the conversation that he did not like. She would never have let it drop otherwise.

When Bruno and I were alone together we never discussed our families. We wandered around the village but never strayed too far from his grazing cows. To have adventures we explored abandoned buildings. In Grana there were more of these than even we could have wished for: old stables, old haylofts and granaries, an old shop with its dust-covered, empty shelves, an ancient bread oven blackened by smoke. Everywhere there was the same kind of detritus that I had seen at the mill, as if for a good while after these buildings had fallen into disuse someone had been occupying them, badly, until they were abandoned for good. In some kitchens we would find a table and a bench still in place, a plate or one or two glasses in the larder, a frying pan still hanging above the fireplace. Fourteen people were living in Grana in 1984, but in the past there had been as many as one hundred.

The village was dominated by a building that was more modern and imposing than the houses that surrounded it: it had three white-plastered floors, an external staircase, and a courtyard enclosed by a wall that had collapsed at one point. We got in through there, stepping over the weeds that had invaded the courtyard. The door on the ground floor had only been pulled to, and when Bruno pushed it we found ourselves in a shadowy entrance hall, complete with benches and a wooden coat rack. I realized immediately where we were, perhaps because all schools resemble one another: but the school in Grana was being used now only to rear the fat, gray rabbits that peered at us fearfully from a row of cages. The schoolroom smelled of hay, animal feed, urine, and of wine that was turning to vinegar. On a wooden dais, where in the past a lectern must have stood, some empty tins had been thrown; but nobody had had the temerity to take down the crucifix from the far wall, or to make firewood from the desks that had been pushed up against it.

These were more interesting to me than the rabbits. I went to have a closer look: they were long and narrow, each with four holes for inkwells, their wood polished by all the hands that had rested there. Inside, with a knife or a nail, those same hands had carved a few letters. Initials. The G for Guglielmina appeared frequently.

"Do you know who they are?"

"Some of them, yes," Bruno said. "Some of them I don't know, but I've heard of them."

"But when was this?"

"I don't know. This school's always been closed."

I did not get a chance to ask any more questions before we heard Bruno's aunt calling. It was thus that all of our adventures ended: the peremptory command arrived, shouted once, twice, a third time, reaching us wherever we happened to be. Bruno snorted. Then he said goodbye and rushed off. He would drop everything unfinished—a game, a conversation—and I knew that I would not see him again that day.

I stayed a little longer in the old school: I examined every desk, read all the initials, and tried to imagine the names of the children. Then, snooping further I found a more cleanly cut and recently made carving. The grooves left by the knife stood out against the gray wood as if freshly cut. I ran a finger over the G and over the B, and it was impossible to have any doubt as to the identity of their author. And so I made a connection between other things, things that I had seen but not understood in the ruins of the buildings that Bruno would take me to, and I began to understand something about the secret life of that ghost village.

• • •

July was flying past meanwhile. The grass mowed at our arrival had grown back a foot, and along the mule track the herds passed, heading for the high pastures. I would watch them disappearing up the deep valley, hearing the sound of their hooves and bells as they made their way through the woods, reappearing after a while in the distance above the treeline, like flocks of birds alighted on the mountainside. Two evenings a week my mother and I would take the path in the opposite direction, towards another village—one that was scarcely more than a handful of houses at the bottom of the valley. It would take us half an hour to arrive there on foot, and at the end of the path it seemed as if we had suddenly re-entered the modern world. The lights of a bar illuminated the bridge across the river, cars could be seen going to and fro on the trunk road, and the music blended with the voices of villagers sitting outside. Down there it was hotter, and the summer was both lively and leisurely, like summers at the seaside. A group of young men was gathered around tables: they were smoking, laughing, every so often one was picked up by passing friends, and they would drive off together towards the bar higher up the valley. My mother and I, on the other hand, would join the queue for the payphone. We would wait our turn before going together into that cabin exhausted by conversations. My parents would keep it short: even at home they were not inclined to small talk; listening to them was like overhearing old friends who needed few words to understand each other.

"So, mountain man," he would say. "How's it going? Climbed any good peaks lately?"

"Not yet. But I'm in training."

"Good for you. And how's your friend?"

"He's fine. But he's going up to the *alpeggio* soon, so I won't be seeing him anymore. It takes an hour to get there."

"Well, an hour away isn't so far. I guess we'll have to go and see him together. What do you think?"

"I'd like that. When are you coming?"

"In August," my father would say. And before signing off he

would add: "Give a kiss to your mother from me. And look after her, do you hear? Don't let her get lonely."

I would promise him that I would, but secretly thought that he was the one feeling alone. I could imagine him in Milan, in the empty apartment with the windows wide open to the noise of traffic. My mother was doing fine; she was happy. We would go back to Grana by the same path through the woods, over which darkness had now fallen. She would turn on a torch and direct it at her feet. She had no fear of the night. Her calmness was such that it reassured me too: we walked following her boots in that uncertain light, and after a while I would hear her singing in a low voice, as if to herself. If I knew the song I would join in, also in a low voice. The sounds of the traffic, the radios, the laughter of the young people gradually vanished behind us. The air became fresher as we climbed. I knew that I was almost there a little before seeing the lit windows, when the wind carried towards us the smell of chimney smoke.

TWO

I DO NOT KNOW what changes my father had detected in me that year, but he had already decided that the time had come to take me with him. He came up from Milan one Saturday, breaking into our routine with his battered Alfa, determined not to waste a minute of his short vacation. He had brought a map that he pinned to the wall, and a felt-tip pen with which he intended to mark routes taken, as generals do with conquests. The old military backpack, his velvet plus fours, the red jumper worn by climbers of the Dolomites: this would be his uniform. My mother preferred not to get involved, seeking refuge with her geraniums and her books. Bruno was already away in the alpine pastures, and all I could do was keep going back to our haunts alone, missing him, so I welcomed this new development: I began to learn my father's way of being in the mountains, the nearest thing to an education that I was to get from him.

We would leave early in the morning, driving up to the villages at the foot of Monte Rosa. They were more fashionable tourist spots than our own, and with sleep-filled eyes I saw rush past the strings of little villas, the hotels built in an "Alpine" style in the early twentieth century, the ugly condominiums of the sixties, the caravan sites along the river. The whole valley was still in shadow and wet with dew. My father drank a coffee in the first open bar, then flung his rucksack over his shoulder with the seriousness of an Alpine infantryman. The path would start behind a church, or after a wooden footbridge, then enter the woods and immediately steepen. Before taking it I would look up at the sky. Above our heads the glaciers sparkled, illuminated by the sun; the early morning cold raised the hairs on my arms.

On the path my father would let me walk in front. He would keep a step behind me, so that when necessary I could hear what he was saying, and hear his breathing. I had rules to follow, few but clear: one, establish a pace and keep to it without stopping; two, no talking; three, when faced with a fork in the way, always choose the uphill route. He puffed and panted more than I did, on account of his smoking and his sedentary office life, but for at least an hour he would not countenance a break; not to get our breath back, or to drink, or to look at anything. The woods were of no interest, in his eyes. It was my mother, in our wanderings around Grana, who would point out plants and trees and teach me their names, as if each one was a person with its own character; but for my father the woods merely provided access to the mountains: we climbed through them with our heads down, concentrating on the rhythm of our walking—of our legs, lungs, and hearts—in mute, private communion with our own exertions. Underfoot there were stones worn down over centuries by the passage of animals and men. Sometimes we would pass a wooden cross, or a bronze plaque engraved with a name, or a shrine with a small Madonna and some flowers, giving to those corners of the wood the somber atmosphere of a cemetery. And then the silence between us assumed a different character, as if this was the only respectful way to pass by them.

I would only look up when the trees ended. On the flank of the glacier the path became less steep, and emerging into the sun, we would come across the last of the high villages. These were abandoned or semi-abandoned places, in even worse condition than Grana, except for the odd isolated stable, a fountain that still worked, a chapel that was still maintained. Above and below the houses the ground had been flattened and the stones collected in piles, and then ditches had been dug to irrigate and fertilize and the banks of the river terraced so as to make fields and vegetable gardens: my father would show me these works and speak with admiration of the old mountain people. Those that had arrived from the north of the Alpine region during the Middle Ages were capable of cultivating land where no one else had ventured before. They had special techniques, as well as a special resistance to the cold and to deprivation. Nowadays, he said, no one could survive the winter up there, completely self-sufficient for food and for everything else, as these people had managed to do for centuries.

I looked at the crumbling houses and tried hard to imagine their inhabitants. I couldn't even begin to understand how anyone could have chosen such a hard life. When I asked my father he answered in his usual enigmatic way: it always seemed as if he could not give me a solution, but only a few clues instead, so that I would only arrive at the truth through my own efforts.

He said: "They didn't really choose it. If someone comes up this high, it's because down below they won't leave them in peace."

"And who is bothering them there, down below?"

"Landlords. Armies. Priests. Bosses. It depends."

I could tell from the tone of his reply that he wasn't being entirely serious. Now he was bathing his neck with water from the fountain, and was already more cheerful than he had been first thing that morning. He shook the water from his head, wrung it from his beard, and looked up above. In the deep valleys that awaited us there was nothing impeding our view, and sooner or later we would notice someone further up ahead of us on the path. He had an eye as sharp as a hunter's with which to pick out those small red or yellow dots—the color of a rucksack or of an anorak. The more distant they were, the more mocking the tone with which he would ask, pointing to them: "What do you think, Pietro, shall we catch them?"

"Sure," I would answer, wherever they were.

Then our climb would be transformed into a pursuit. Our muscles were well warmed up, and we still had energy to burn. We were ascending through the August pastures, past isolated *alpeggi*, herds of indifferent cows, dogs that came growling around our ankles, and swathes of nettles that stung my bare legs.

"Cut across," my father would say, where the path took a slope too gentle for his liking. "Go straight. Go up this way."

Eventually the incline would steepen, and it was there on those merciless concluding slopes that we would catch our prey. Two or three men, about his age and dressed just like him. They confirmed my sense that there was something from another era about this way of going into the mountains, and that it obeyed outmoded codes. Even the manner they adopted when giving way to us had something ceremonious about it: they would step aside, to the edge of the path, and come to a standstill in order to let us pass. They had no doubt seen us coming, had tried to keep ahead of us, and were not pleased at being caught.

"Good day to you," one would say. "The boy sure can run, no?"

"He sets the pace," my father would reply. "I just follow."

"What I'd give to have legs like his."

"That's right. But we did have once."

"Oh sure. Decades ago maybe. Are you going right to the top?"

"If we can make it."

"Good luck," one of them would say, and with that the exchange was concluded.

We would move off in silence, just as we had arrived. Gloating was not allowed, but a little while later, when we were a good distance away, I would feel a hand on my shoulder; just a hand touching and pressing, and that was all.

Perhaps it's true, as my mother maintained, that each of us has a favorite altitude in the mountains, a landscape that resembles us, where we feel best. Hers was no doubt that of the woods at fifteen hundred meters, that of the spruce and larch, in the shadow of which the blueberries, junipers, and rhododendrons grow, and the roe deer hide. I was more attracted to the kind of mountainscape that comes afterwards: Alpine meadows, torrents, wetlands, high-altitude herbs, grazing animals. Higher up again the vegetation disappears; snow covers everything until the beginning of summer; and the prevailing color is that of the gray rock, veined with quartz and the yellow of lichen. That was where my father's world began. After three hours' walking the meadows and woods would give way to scree, to lakes hidden in glacial basins, to gorges gouged by avalanches, to streams of icy water. The mountain was transformed into a harsher place, inhospitable and pure: up there he would become happy. He was rejuvenated, perhaps, going back to other mountains and other times. His very step seemed lighter, to have regained a lost agility.

I, on the other hand, was exhausted. Exertion and the lack of oxygen tightened my stomach and made me feel sick. This nausea made every meter a struggle. My father was incapable of noticing: approaching three thousand meters the path became less distinct; on the scree there remained only stone cairns and signs daubed in paint; and he would finally take his place at the head of the expedition. He wouldn't look round to check on how I was. If he did turn, it was only so as to shout out: "Look!" pointing out, on the ridge of the crest above, the horns of the ibexes who were keeping an eye on us, like guardians of that mineral world. Looking up, the summit still seemed very far off to me. My nostrils were filled with the smell of frozen snow and flint.

The end of this torture would arrive unexpectedly. I would make one last leap, go round a rocky outcrop, and suddenly find myself before a pile of stones, or a lightning-stricken iron cross—my father's rucksack flung on the ground, beyond it nothing but sky. It was more of a relief than a cause for elation. There was no reward awaiting us up there: apart from the fact that we could climb no further, there was nothing really special about the summit. I would have been happier reaching a river, or a village.

On the summit my father became reflective. He would take off his shirt and vest and hang them on the cross to dry. It was only on rare occasions that I saw him like this, and bare-chested his body had something vulnerable about it—with his reddened forearms, his strong white shoulders, the small gold chain that he never took off, his neck also red and covered in dust. We would sit down to eat bread and cheese, and to contemplate the panoramic view. In front of us stood the entire massif of Monte Rosa, so close that we could make out the refuges, the cable cars, the artificial lakes, the long procession of roped figures on their way back from the Margherita Hut. My father would then unstop his canteen of wine and smoke his single morning cigarette.

"It isn't called Rosa because it's pink," he would say. "It comes from an old word for ice. The ice mountain."

Then he would list the "four-thousanders"—the peaks above four thousand meters—from east to west, saying them over again because before going there it was important to know them, to have cultivated a long-standing desire for them: the modest Punta Giordani, the Piramide Vincent towering over it, the Balmenhorn on which the great Christ of the Summits rises, the Parrot, with an outline so gentle that it's almost invisible; then the noble peaks of the three sharp-pointed sisters—Gnifetti, Zumstein, and Dufour; the two Lyskamm with the ridge that joins them, the "Devourer of Men"; and at the end the elegantly curved profile of Castor, the rugged Pollux, the deeply carved Black Rock, the Breithorn with its seemingly innocuous air. Finally, to the west, sculpted and solitary, the Matterhorn, which my father called the *Big Nose*, as if it were an elderly aunt of his. He did not willingly turn south, towards the plains: down there the August haze hung heavily, and somewhere beneath that gray blanket Milan was sweltering.

"It all looks so small, doesn't it?" he would say, and I did not understand. I could not understand in what possible sense that magisterial panorama could seem small to him. Perhaps it was other things that seemed small, things that came back to him when he was up there. But his melancholy did not last for long. His cigarette finished, he would extract himself from the mire of his thoughts, collect his things and say: "Shall we go?"

We took the descent at a run, going down every slope at breakneck speed, letting out war cries and American Indian howls, and in less than two hours would be soaking our feet in some village fountain.

• • •

In Grana my mother had made progress with her investigations. I would often spot her in the field where Bruno's mother spent her days. If you glanced up in that direction you would always see her there, a bony woman wearing a yellow beret, bent over, tending her onions and potatoes. She never exchanged a word with anyone, and no one would seek her out there until my mother decided to do so: one of them in the allotment, the other sitting on a tree stump nearby. From a distance it seemed as if they had been chatting there for hours.

"So she does speak then," said my father, who had heard from us about this strange woman.

"Of course she speaks. I've never known anyone who was mute," my mother replied.

"More's the pity," he remarked, but she wasn't in the mood for jokes. She had discovered that Bruno had not advanced beyond primary school that year, and she was furious about it. He had not been to school since April. It was clear that if no one intervened then his education was already at an end, and this was the kind of thing that made my mother indignant, every bit as much in a small mountain village as in Milan.

"You can't always be rescuing everyone," my father said.

"But someone rescued you, or am I wrong?"

"True enough. But then I had to rescue myself from them."

"But you did get to study. They didn't force you to herd cows when you were eleven years old. At eleven you should be going to school."

"I'm just saying that it's different in this case. He does have parents, luckily."

"Some luck," my mother concluded, and my father did not respond. They almost never touched upon the subject of his own childhood, and on those rare occasions he would shake his head and let the subject drop.

And so it was that we were sent, my father and I, as an advance party to forge links with the men of the Guglielmina family. The *alpeggio* or farmstead where they spent the summer consisted of a group of three mountain shacks about an hour's distance from Grana along the track that climbed up the deep valley. We caught sight of them from a distance, perched on its right flank, where the mountain became less steep just before plunging down again until it reached the same stream that flowed through the village. I was already very fond of that little river. I was pleased to meet up with it again there. At this point the valley seemed to close, as if an immense landslide had blocked it upstream, and it ended in a basin watered by small streams and overrun with ferns, bushes of rhubarb, and nettles. Passing through it the way became boggy. Then, leaving behind the wetland, the path went beyond the river and climbed into the sunshine and onto dry ground, towards the huts. From the river onwards all the pastures were well maintained.

"Hey," said Bruno. "It's about time."

"I'm sorry. I had to spend some time with my father."

"Is that your father? What's he like?"

"I don't know," I said. "He's fine."

I had started talking like him. We hadn't seen each other in fifteen days, and we felt like old friends. My father greeted him as if he were one, and even Bruno's uncle made an effort to seem hospitable: he disappeared into one of the huts and came out with a piece of *toma* cheese, some *mocetta* salami, and a flask of wine, but his face hardly accorded with these gestures of welcome. He was a man who seemed marked by his own worst inner thoughts, as if they were carved there in his features. He had an unkempt, bristling, and almost white beard, its moustache thicker and gray; eyebrows that were arched permanently, giving him a distrusting air; and eyes that were sky blue. The hand my father stretched out had taken him by surprise, and the movement he made to shake it seemed hesitant, unnatural; only when unstopping the wine and filling the glasses did he seem back on his own familiar territory.

Bruno had something to show me, so we left them to their drinks and went for a wander around. I took in the farmstead that he had told me so much about. It exuded an ancient dignity—whose presence you could still feel in the drystone walls, in certain enormous angular stones, in the hand-hewn roof beams—as well as a more recent air of poverty, like a layer of grease and dust over everything. The longest of the cabins was being used as a cowshed, humming with flies and encrusted with dung right up to its threshold. In the second, its broken windows stopped with bits of rag and its roof patched with metal sheets, Luigi Guglielmina and his heirs lived. The third was the cellar: Bruno took me to see it rather than the room in which he slept. Even in Grana he had never invited me into his home.

He said: "I'm learning how to make the *toma*."

"Meaning what?"

"The cheese. Come."

The cellar surprised me. It was cool and shadowy, the only really clean place in the whole *alpeggio*. The thick shelves made of larch had been recently washed: the cheeses were being aged there, their crusts moistened with brine. They were so polished, round, and symmetrical as to seem laid out in display for some kind of competition.

"Did you make them?" I asked.

"No, no. For now I only turn them and that's it. They're nice ones, no?"

"What do you mean *turn* them?"

"Once every week I turn them over and sprinkle them with salt. Then I wash everything down and tidy up in here."

"They're really nice ones," I said.

Outside, on the other hand, lay plastic buckets, a pile of half-rotted wood, a stove made out of a diesel oil drum, a bathtub converted into a drinking trough, scattered potato peelings, and the odd bone picked clean by the dogs. It wasn't just an absence of decorum: there was a perceptible contempt for things, a certain kind of pleasure in mistreating them and letting them go to pot that I had also begun to recognize in Grana. It was as if these places had already had their fate sealed, that it was a waste of time and effort to try to maintain them.

My father and Bruno's uncle were already on their second glass, and we found them in the midst of a discussion about the economics of small Alpine farmsteads. My father must have initiated the conversation. When it came to other people's lives he was more interested in their work than anything else: how many head of cattle, how many liters of milk a day, what the yield was like regarding the production of cheese. Luigi Guglielmina was more than happy to discuss it with someone who knew what they were talking about, and he made his calculations out loud to show that, what with current prices and the absurd regulations imposed by cattle breeders, his work no longer made economic sense, and was continued by him only because of his passion for it.

He said: "When I die, within ten years it will all revert to forest up here. Then they'll be happy."

"Don't your children like this kind of work?" my father asked.

"Oh sure. What they don't like is working their asses off."

What struck me most was not hearing him talk in such terms, but his prophecy. It had never occurred to me that the pastures had once been wooded, and that they could revert to being so again. I looked at the cows scattered over the grazing, and made an effort to imagine these fields colonized by the first thick covering of weeds and shrubs, erasing every sign of what had once been there. The drainage ditches, the drystone walls, the paths, eventually even the houses themselves.

Bruno had in the meantime lit the fire in the open-air stove. Without waiting to be told, he went to the bath to fill a saucepan with water and began to peel potatoes with his penknife. There were so many things that he knew how to do: he made a pasta dish and put it on the table with the boiled potatoes, the *toma*, the *mocetta*, and the wine. At that point his cousins appeared: two tall and thickset youths, about twenty-five years old, who sat down to eat with their heads lowered, looked up at us briefly, and then went off for a siesta. Bruno's uncle watched them going, and in the grimace contorting his lips it was clear to see that he despised them.

My father paid no heed to such things. At the end of the meal he stretched, put his hands behind his head, and looked at the sky, as if he was about to enjoy a show. And he said as much: "What a show." His vacation was nearly over, and he had already started to look at the mountains with nostalgia. He would no longer be able to make it to certain summits that year. We had some above us: all scree, spurs, pinnacles, rivers of fallen rock, gullies of debris, and broken ridges. They looked like the ruins of an immense fortress destroyed by cannon fire, poised precariously before collapsing completely: what could indeed be considered a real show, in fact, for someone like my father.

"What are these mountains called?" he asked. A strange question, I thought, given the amount of time he spent poring over his wall map.

Bruno's uncle glanced up as if he were looking for signs of rain, and with a vague gesture said: "Grenon."

"Which one is Grenon?"

"This one. For us it's the mountain of Grana."

"All of these peaks together?"

"Of course. We don't give names to peaks here. It's the region." Having eaten and drunk he was beginning to get fed up with having us around.

"Have you ever been there?" my father persisted. "Right up to the heights I mean."

"When I was young. I used to go with my father, hunting."

"And have you been to the glacier?"

"No. I never had the chance. But I would've liked to," he admitted.

"I'm thinking of going up there tomorrow," my father said. "I'm taking the boy to trample some snow. If it's all right with you, we could take yours with us too."

This is what my father had been aiming at all along. Luigi Guglielmina took a moment to understand what he was saying. *Yours*? Then he remembered Bruno who was there beside me—we were playing with one of the dogs, one of that year's puppies. But we were also hanging on every word.

"Do you feel like going?" he asked.

"Oh yes," said Bruno.

The uncle frowned. He was more used to saying no than yes.

But perhaps he felt cornered by this stranger, or who knows, perhaps for once he felt sorry for the boy.

"Well, go then," he said. Then he put the cork in the bottle and got up from the table, tired now of the effort to appear anything other than who he was.

The glacier fascinated the scientist in my father before it did the climber. It reminded him of his studies in physics and chemistry, of the mythology by which he was formed. The next day, as we climbed towards the Mezzalama refuge, he told us a story which resembled one of those myths: the glacier, he said, is the memory of past winters which the mountain safeguards for us. Above a certain altitude it stores the memory, and if we wish to know about a winter in the distant past, it's up there that we need to go.

"It's called *the level of permanent snow cover*," he explained. "It's where the summer cannot melt all of the snow that falls in winter. Some of it lasts until autumn, and is buried beneath the snow of the next winter. Therefore it's saved. Under the new snow, little by little, it gradually turns to ice. It adds a layer to the growth of the glacier, just like growth rings in tree trunks, and by counting them we can know how old it is. Except that a glacier doesn't just stand there on top of the mountain. It moves. All the time it does nothing but slide downwards."

"Why?" I asked.

"Why do you think?"

"Because it's heavy," said Bruno.

"Exactly," my father said. "The glacier is heavy, and the rock beneath it is very smooth. That's why it slides down. Slowly, but without ever stopping. It slides down the mountain until it reaches a level that's too warm for it. We call that the *melt level*. Can you see it there, down below?"

We were walking on a moraine that seemed made of sand. A spit of ice and rubble jutted out beneath us, way down below the path. It was crisscrossed by rivulets that collected into a small lake which was opaque, metallic, icy-looking.

"That water down there," my father said, "it hasn't come from the snow that fell this year. It's from snow that the mountain has stored for who knows how long. Perhaps it's from snow that fell a hundred winters ago."

"A hundred? Really?" asked Bruno.

"Perhaps even more. It's difficult to determine exactly. You'd need to know the exact degree of incline and friction. You can try an experiment first."

"How?"

"Ah, that's easy. Do you see those crevasses up there above? Tomorrow we'll go there, throw in a coin, then go and sit in the river and wait for it to arrive."

My father laughed. Bruno continued looking at the crevasses and at the glacier where it jutted below, and you could tell that he was fascinated by the idea. For my part I was not so interested in bygone winters. I could feel in the pit of my stomach that we were about to go beyond the level at which, on previous occasions, our ascent had come to an end. The timing was also unusual: in the afternoon we had felt a few drops of rain, and now with evening falling we were heading into fog. It felt very strange to discover, at the end of the moraine, a wooden building on two stories. The smell of fumes from a generator announced its proximity, followed by voices shouting in a language I did not recognize. The wooden platform at the entrance, pockmarked by crampons, was cluttered with rucksacks, ropes, sweaters, vests, and thick socks hung out everywhere to dry; and by climbers crossing it in unlaced boots, carrying their washing.

That evening the refuge was full. No one would be turned away, but some would have to sleep on benches, or even on tables. Bruno and I were the youngest members of this gathering by far; we were amongst the first to eat, and to make room for others to do so we went immediately upstairs afterwards to the large dorm where we would be sharing a bed. Up there, fully dressed under a rough blanket, we spent a long while waiting for sleep to come. Through the window we could not see the stars or the gleam of the lights in the valley below, only the burning ends of the cigarettes of those who went outside for a smoke. We listened to the men on the ground floor: after supper they were comparing itineraries for the next day, discussing the uncertain weather conditions and recounting other nights spent in refuges, and old exploits made from them. My father had ordered a liter of wine and joined the others, and every so often I could make out his voice. Despite not having any conquest of summits in prospect, he had nevertheless made a name for himself as the guy who was taking two young boys up a glacier, and the role filled him with pride. He had encountered several people from his own neck of the woods and was exchanging jokes with them in Veneto dialect. Being shy, I felt embarrassed for him.

Bruno said: "Your father knows a thing or two, doesn't he?"

"He sure does," I said.

"It's good that he teaches you about it."

"Why, doesn't yours?"

"I don't know. It always seems like I irritate him."

I thought to myself that my father was good at talking but that listening was not his strong point. Nor was paying much attention to me, otherwise he would have noticed how I was feeling: I had struggled to eat, and it would have been better to have had nothing, tormented as I now was by nausea. The smell of soup rising from the kitchen was making things worse. I was taking deep breaths to calm my stomach, and Bruno noticed: "Are you not feeling well?"

"Not really."

"Would you like me to call your father?"

"No, no. It'll go away in a minute."

I was keeping my stomach warm with my hands. I would have liked more than anything to be in my own bed, and to hear my mother nearby in front of the stove. We remained in silence until at ten the supervisor announced lights-out and turned off the generator, plunging the refuge into darkness. A little while later we saw the light from the head torches of men coming upstairs in search of somewhere to sleep. My father also passed by, the grappa heavy on his breath, to see how we were: I kept my eyes shut and pretended to be asleep.

• • •

In the morning we left before daybreak. Now the fog filled the valleys below us and the sky was clear, the color of mother-of-pearl, with the last stars slowly fading out as the light spread. We had not anticipated dawn by much: the mountaineers heading for the most distant peaks had already left some time ago; we had heard them fumbling in the middle of the night and could now see some of them roped together high up, nothing more than miniature shipwrecks in a sea of white.

My father attached for us the crampons that he had hired, and roped us together at a length of five meters from each other: himself first, then Bruno, then me. He strapped our chests with a complicated arrangement of the rope around our anoraks, but he hadn't tied such knots for years and our preparation turned out to be long-winded and laborious. We ended up being the last to leave the refuge: we had still to cover a stretch of scree which our crampons knocked against and tended to get stuck in, and the rope hampered my movement and made me feel clumsy, burdened with too much gear. But everything changed the moment I set foot on snow. From my baptism on the glacier I remember this: an unexpected strength in my legs, the steel points biting through the hard snow, the crampons that gripped to perfection.

I had woken feeling reasonably well, but after a while the warmth from the refuge dissipated, and the nausea began to grow. Up ahead my father was pulling the group on. I could see that he was in a hurry. Although he had claimed that he only wanted to have a short excursion, I suspected that he harbored a secret hope of reaching some peak or other, surprising the other climbers by turning up at the summit with the two of us in tow. But I was struggling. Between one step and the next it was as if a hand was wringing my stomach. Whenever I stopped to get my breath the rope between myself and Bruno tautened, forcing him to stop as well, the tension then reaching my father who would turn around to look at me, annoyed.

"What's going on?" he asked. He thought that I was playing up. "Let's get a move on."

As the sun rose three black shadows appeared on the glacier next to us. Then the snow lost its bluish tinge and became blindingly white, and almost immediately afterwards began to give way beneath our crampons. The clouds below us were swelling with the heat of the morning, and even I understood that soon they would rise up as they had the day before. The idea of reaching anywhere was becoming more and more unrealistic, but my father was not the kind of person to admit the fact and withdraw: on the contrary, he was stubbornly determined to plow on. At a certain point we encountered a crevasse; he gauged its width carefully by eye and with one determined step got across it, planted the ice pick in the snow and wound the rope around it to reel Bruno in.

I no longer had any interest in what we were doing. The sunrise, the glacier, the chain of summits that surrounded us, the clouds that separated us from the world: I was indifferent to all of this otherworldly beauty. All I wanted was for someone to tell me how much further we had to walk. I got to the edge of the crevasse where Bruno, in front of me, was leaning out to look into it. My father told him to take a deep breath and to jump. While waiting for my turn I looked around: beneath us on one side the mountain's incline became sheerer, and the glacier split in a steep serac; beyond the wreck of broken, collapsed, and piled up blocks, the refuge from where we had started out was being engulfed by fog. It seemed to me now that we would never get back, and when I looked at Bruno for support he was already on the other side of the crevasse. My father was slapping him on the back, congratulating him on the jump that he had executed. Not I, I would never be able to get across; my stomach gave in, and I threw up my breakfast onto the snow. And so it was that my altitude sickness was no longer a secret.

My father became frightened. He rushed to my aid in alarm, jumping back across the crevasse and in doing so tangling the ropes that held the three of us together. His fear surprised me—I had expected his anger instead—but at the time I had not realized the risks he had taken by leading us up there: eleven years old, poorly equipped and pursued by bad weather, we were being dragged up the glacier by his obstinacy. He knew that the only cure for altitude sickness was to go down to a lower level, and he did not hesitate before starting the descent. He reversed the order on the rope so that I could walk ahead and stop when I felt unwell: there was nothing left in my stomach, but every so often I was convulsed by dry retching, spitting out drool.

Soon we were entering the fog. From his end of the rope my father asked: "How are you feeling? Do you have a headache?"

"I don't think so."

"And how's your stomach?"

"A bit better," I answered, though what I felt above all was weak.

"Take this," said Bruno. He gave me a handful of snow that he had compressed in his fist until it had turned to ice. I tried sucking it. Thanks partly to this, and partly to the relief afforded by the descent, my stomach began to calm down.

It was a morning in August in 1984, the last memory I have of that summer: the next day Bruno would return to the high pastures, and my father to Milan. But at that moment the three of us were on the glacier, together, in a way that would never happen again, with a rope that joined each of us to another, whether we wanted it to or not.

I kept stumbling over the crampons and could not walk straight. Bruno was immediately behind me, and soon I heard above the sound of our footsteps in the snow his *Oh, oh, oh*. It was the call with which he brought the cows back to the stable. *Eh, eh, eh. Oh, oh, oh*. He was using it to bring me back to the refuge, given that I could hardly stay on my feet by now: I abandoned myself to his song and let my legs adopt its rhythm and in that way no longer had to think about anything.

"But did you look into the crevasse?" he asked. "Holy shit it was deep."

I did not answer. I still had in my eyes the image I had seen of them there, so close and triumphant, like father and son. In front of me now the fog and the snow formed a uniform whiteness, and I was concentrating only on not falling. Bruno said nothing else, and resumed his chanting.

THREE

WINTER, DURING THOSE YEARS, became for me the season of nostalgia. My father detested skiers and would not countenance mingling with them: there was something offensive to him in the game of going down the mountain without the effort required to climb it first, along a slope smoothed by snowcats and equipped with a ski lift. He despised them because they arrived in herds and left behind them nothing but ruins. Sometimes in the summer we would come across the pylon of a chairlift, or the remains of a caterpillar track stuck on a threadbare piste, or what was left of a disused cable station at altitude, a rusted wheel on a block of cement in the middle of scree.

"What this really needs is a bomb under it," my father would say. And he was not joking.

It was the same frame of mind with which he would watch at Christmas the news items devoted to skiing holidays. Thousands of people from the cities invaded the Alpine valleys, got into queues at those stations, and hurtled down our paths—and he would disassociate himself from it all, locking himself away in the apartment in Milan. My mother once suggested that we should take a day trip to Grana, so that I could see it in the snow, and my father replied tersely: "No." He wouldn't like it. In the winter the mountain was not fit for humankind, and should be given a wide berth. According to his philosophy of ascending and coming down, or of going up above to escape the things that tormented you below, the climbing season needed to be followed by one of seriousness—by the period of work, of life on the flat, and of black moods.

In this way I too began to feel nostalgia for being in the mountains, the affliction to which I had seen him subjected for years without understanding its cause. Now I too found myself capable of becoming spellbound when La Grigna appeared at the end of an avenue. I would reread the pages of the Alpine Club Guide as if it were a personal diary, drinking in its antiquated prose, and it would give to me the illusion of retracing the paths it described step by step: *climbing up steep grassy ridges to reach a neglected Alp . . . and from here, proceeding through scattered boulders and the residual ice field . . . to then attain the crest of the summit in the proximity of a pronounced depression.* But in the meantime my legs became gradually paler, their scratches and scabs healed, and they forgot the stings of nettles, the icy sensation of fording streams without socks or shoes, and the relief afforded by cool bed sheets after an afternoon in the blazing sun. Nothing, in the winter city, could strike me with the same force. I observed it from behind a filter that rendered it faded and indistinct, just a fog of people and cars that needed to be got through twice a day; and when I looked from the window at the avenue below, the days spent in Grana seemed so far off as to make me question whether they had actually existed. Could I have invented them, just dreamed them up? But I only felt this until I noticed, in a new kind of light on the balcony, in a bud emerging in the grass between two lanes of traffic, that the spring was coming even to Milan, and my nostalgia turned to anticipation of the moment when I would go back up there again.

• • •

Bruno waited with the same excitement for that day to arrive. Except that I came and went, and he stayed. I think that from his vantage point in the fields he must have kept an eye out for our return, since he would come to find us within an hour of our arrival, shouting "Berio!" from the courtyard. This was the nickname with which he had baptized me. "Come on," he would say, not bothering with any kind of greeting, or with saying anything else for that matter, as if we had last seen each other just the day before. And it was true: the intervening months were canceled in an instant, and our friendship seemed to be lived in a single uninterrupted summer.

Yet Bruno, in the meantime, had been growing up more quickly than me. He was almost always covered in dirt from the stables, and refused to come inside the house. He would wait on the balcony, leaning on the balustrade, which we almost never did ourselves, since it would move the moment you touched it, convincing us that one of these days it would collapse. He would look over his shoulder as if checking to see whether he'd been followed: he had absconded from his cows and was taking me away from my books, to have adventures which he did not want to ruin by talking about them.

"Where are we going?" I would ask while lacing my boots.

"Into the mountains," he would limit himself to saying, with a mocking tone that he had developed, perhaps the same tone that he used when answering his uncle. He was smiling. All I needed to do was to trust him. My mother trusted me, and would often enough repeat that she didn't worry because she knew that I would do nothing wrong. Nothing "wrong"—rather than reckless or stupid—as if she was alluding to quite other dangers that would come my way in life. She did not resort to prohibitions or to other advice before letting us leave.

Going into the mountains with Bruno had nothing to do with the peaks. Although we did follow a path into the woods, climbing quickly for half an hour, we would at some point known only to him leave the beaten track and continue along other routes. Up a gorge even, or through the thickest fir cover. It was a mystery to me how he got his bearings. He walked fast, following an internal map which indicated passageways where all I could see was a collapsed bank or a scar that looked too steep. But right at the last moment, between two twisted pines, the rock would reveal a fissure that we could get a purchase on to climb, and a ledge, which had been invisible at first, would allow us to cross it with ease. Some of these trails had been first opened up with the blows of pickaxes. When I asked him who had used them he would say, "the miners," or, alternatively: "the woodcutters," pointing out the telltale signs that I was incapable of noticing. The winding gear of a cable lift, rusted and overgrown with weeds. The earth that beneath a drier layer was still blackened by fire, where a charcoal works had been. The woods were littered with these excavations, mounds, and ruins, which Bruno interpreted for me as if they were phrases written in a dead language. Together with these cryptic signs he would teach me a dialect that I found less abstract than Italian: as soon as I was in the mountains it was as if I would need to substitute the concrete language of things for the abstract language of books, now that the things themselves were tangible and I could touch them with my own hands. The larch: *la brenga*. The spruce: *la pezza*; the Swiss pine: *l'arula*. An overhanging rock under which to take cover from the rain was a *barma*. A stone was a *berio*—and so was I, Pietro. I was very fond of that nickname. Every river cut a valley and so was called a *valey*; every valley had two sides with contrasting characteristics: an *adret* nicely exposed to the sun, where there were villages and fields, and an *envers* that was damp and in shadow, left to the forest and to wildlife. But of the two it was this reverse side that we preferred.

There no one could disturb us and we could go hunting for treasure. There really were mines in the woods surrounding Grana: tunnels closed off, boarded up with a few planks that had already been trespassed through before us. In the old times, according to

Bruno, they had found gold there, searching for seams all over the mountains. But they had not managed to extract everything. Surely there must be a little remaining. And so we would enter into blind tunnels which ended in nothing after a few meters. And into others that went deep and were winding and pitch black inside. The ceilings were so low as to make it difficult to walk upright. The water that dripped down the walls gave the impression that the whole thing might cave in at any moment: I knew how dangerous it was, and I also knew that I was betraying my mother's trust, since there was nothing very sensible about poking around in such death-traps—the sense of guilt I felt ruined any pleasure there might have been in doing so. I longed to be like Bruno, to have the courage to rebel openly and to accept any punishment that might follow, with my head held high. Instead I disobeyed furtively, and was ashamed of what I had got away with. I would think about these things as my feet were soaked by the puddles of water in there. We never did find gold: sooner or later the tunnels turned out to have been blocked by a cave-in, or just became too dark to go along any further, and there was no choice but to retreat.

We made up for the disappointment by ransacking some ruins on the way home. Shepherds' huts that we came across in the woods, constructed from whatever came to hand there, resembling burrows. Bruno would pretend to be discovering them with me. I suspect that he knew every one of those overgrown cabins, but it was more fun to be shoulder-barging open their doors as if for the first time. Inside we would purloin a dented bowl or the terminally blunted blade of a scythe, and imagine them to be valuable finds—and in the village, before parting, we would divide the spoils.

In the evening my mother would ask me where we had been.

"Just around here," I would answer, with a shrug. In front of the stove I did not give her much satisfaction now.

"Did you find anything worth seeing?"

"Of course, Mum. The woods."

She would give me a melancholy look, as if she were losing me. She really believed that the silence between two people was the origin of all their troubles.

"All I want to know is that you are OK," she would say, giving up and abandoning me to my thoughts.

• • •

In the other battle she was fighting at Grana she held firm. From the beginning she had taken Bruno's education to heart, like a personal crusade, but she knew full well that she could achieve nothing on her own: she needed to forge alliances with the women of his family. She had understood that his mother would be of no help at all, so she concentrated her efforts on his aunt. This is how my mother operated: knocking on doors and gaining entrance to homes, returning in a friendly but determined manner, not relenting until the aunt eventually committed to sending him to school during the winter—and over to our place to do homework in the summer. This was already quite an achievement. I don't know what the uncle thought about the matter; perhaps up there in the *alpeggio* he was cursing the lot of us. Or perhaps, in truth, nobody in that family really cared anything about the boy.

And so it is that I remember long hours spent with Bruno in our kitchen doing history and geography revision, while outside the woods and the river and the sky beckoned. He would be sent to us three times a week, scrubbed and well dressed for the occasion. My mother would get him to read aloud from my books—Stevenson, Verne, Twain, Jack London—and would leave them with him after the lesson so that he could continue practicing while he was up in the pastures. Bruno liked reading novels, but studying grammar always sent him into a crisis: for him it was like studying a foreign language. And seeing how he got entangled with the rules of Italian, failing to spell a word correctly or stuttering over a conjunction, I felt humiliated on his behalf and annoyed with my mother. I could not see the justice of what we were forcing him to do. And yet Bruno did not utter a single word of protest or complaint. He understood how much it mattered to her, and perhaps having never experienced before what is was like to matter to someone, he struggled hard to learn.

Only on rare occasions during the summer was he allowed to come walking with us, and these were his holidays, the reward for the efforts that went into his studies: whether it was a summit we were taken to by my father, or just a field where my mother would spread out a blanket for lunch. On these occasions I would see Bruno transformed. Though undisciplined by nature, he would adapt to the rules and the rituals of our family. And whilst with me he already behaved like a grown-up, with my parents he would happily regress to his proper age. He allowed my mother to feed him, to dress him, to caress him—while my father inspired in him a respect that bordered on adulation. I could see it in the way he would follow behind him on the path, and how he would listen in rapt silence when my father started explaining something. These were perfectly ordinary moments in the life of a family, but Bruno had never experienced anything like them—and part of me felt proud of them, as if they were gifts that I myself had bestowed on him. On the other hand I would sometimes watch him with my father to try to gauge the nature of the understanding that there was between them, and I would feel that Bruno would have made a good son for him—perhaps not a better one than I was, but in a certain sense a more suitable one. Bruno was full of questions for him that he would ask naturally, without hesitation. He had the confidence that allowed him to get close to my father, and the physical strength to follow him anywhere. I would think these things but then try to suppress them, as if they were something about which I should be ashamed.

Eventually Bruno passed not only the first grade of senior school but the second and even the third, achieving an "average" mark in the exam. It was such an event in his family that his aunt phoned us immediately in Milan to give us the news. What a peculiar word, I thought, and wondered who had come up with it, since there was nothing "average" about Bruno. My mother on the other hand was simply delighted, and when we went back up to Grana she took him a prize: a box of chisels and gouges for working with wood. Then she began to ask herself what else she could do for him.

• • •

The summer of 1987 arrived: we were fourteen. We spent an entire month dedicated to a systematic exploration of the river. Not from its banks this time, or from the paths that intersected it from the woods, but in the water itself, in the current, jumping from rock to rock or wading within it. We had never heard of canyoning, if such a thing even existed at that time, but did it anyway, albeit in reverse: proceeding upstream from the bridge at Grana, climbing back up the valley. Just above the village we entered a long gorge of calm water, in the shadow of banks densely covered in vegetation. There were large pools infested with insects, tangles of submerged wood, old wary trout that would scatter at our approach. Further up, the gradient became problematic, making the river flow headlong, its progress all leaps and falls. Where we could not manage to scramble over we would rig up a rope to cross the rapids, or use a fallen tree trunk by floating it onto the water and wedging it between rocks to make a pontoon. Sometimes even a single modest waterfall would cost us hours of work. But this is what made the feat special. We planned to negotiate such passages one by one then connect them all, going up the entire length of the river on one glorious day at the end of summer.

First, though, we needed to discover its source. Towards the August bank holiday we had already gone beyond the territory of Bruno's uncle. There was a large tributary which provided the Alpine farmsteads with water, and a little way after this fork a rudimentary bridge consisting of a few planks of wood provided a crossing. After that the river narrowed and presented us with no further difficulty. I understood from the thinning out of the tree cover that we were getting to a level of two thousand meters. The alders and birches disappeared from the banks, all other trees giving way to the larch; above our heads was that world of rock and stone that Luigi Guglielmina had called *Grenon*. At this point the bed of the river lost its usual appearance—that of something excavated and shaped by the water—becoming instead nothing but scree. The water literally vanished beneath our feet. It escaped beneath the stones here, amidst the contorted roots of a juniper.

This is not how I had imagined my river ending up, and I was disappointed. I turned towards Bruno, who was climbing a few steps behind me. All afternoon he had been keeping himself to himself, lost in his own thoughts. When this mood came over him the only thing I could do was follow after him in silence, hoping that it would pass.

But as soon as he caught sight of the spring he snapped out of it. He had sensed my disappointment at a glance. "Wait," he said. He signaled to me to keep quiet and listen, and looked at the scree at our feet.

That day the air was not still, like it was at the height of summer. A cold wind blew over the tepid stones and, passing through the fading plants, carried away soft clusters of seeds and set up a rustling in the trees. By listening hard, together with this rustling I could hear water gurgling. A sound different from the ones it makes above ground, deeper and more muffled. It seemed to be coming from beneath the scree. I understood what it was and began to climb again to follow it, searching like a dowser for the water that I could hear but not see. Bruno let me go on ahead, already knowing what we would find.

What we found was a lake hidden in a basin at the foot of the Grenon. It was circular and at two or three hundred meters across was the largest that I'd ever seen in the mountains. The marvelous thing about Alpine lakes is that you never expect them, while climbing, unless you know already that they are there—that you don't catch sight of them until the very last step over a ridge, at which point the view suddenly opens up before your eyes. The basin was all scree on its sunlit side, and as you moved your gaze gradually towards the shadows you saw that it became covered at first by willows and rhododendrons, and then by more woods. In its middle was this lake. Observing it, I was able to understand how it had been made: the ancient avalanche that could be seen from below, from Bruno's uncle's pastures, had sealed the valley like a dam. The lake had been formed above the dam, collecting the water that ran off from the surrounding snow, before resurfacing downhill, filtered by the scree, becoming in the process the river that we knew. I liked the fact that it was born in this way. It seemed to me an origin worthy of a great river.

"What's this lake called?" I asked.

"I have no idea," Bruno said. "Grenon. Almost everything's called that around here."

His previous mood had returned. He sat down on the grass and I remained standing next to him. It was easier to look at the lake than to look at each other: a few meters in front of us a large rock emerged from the water, like a small island, and it was useful to have something to fix my gaze on.

"Your parents have spoken to my uncle," said Bruno, after a while. "Did you know about that?"

"No," I lied.

"Strange. I don't understand what's going on at all."

"About what?"

"About the secrets you have between you."

"So what did they talk to your uncle about?"

"About me," he replied.

Now I sat down next to him. What he was about to tell me came as no surprise. My parents had been discussing it for some time now, and I had not needed to listen behind doors in order to discover their intentions: the previous day they had suggested to Luigi Guglielmina that in September we should take Bruno with us. Take him to Milan. They had offered to take him into our home, and to enroll him in a college. In a technical or professional institute, whichever he preferred. They were thinking about a trial year: if Bruno wasn't happy with the arrangement he would be able to give up and return to Grana next summer. If on the other hand it all worked out, then they would be happy to keep him with us until his graduation. At that point he would be free to decide what he wanted to do with the rest of his life.

Even in the account of this given by Bruno I could recognize the voice of my mother. *Happy to keep him with us. Free to decide. The rest of his life.*

I said: "Your uncle will never agree to it."

"Oh but he will," said Bruno. "And do you know why?"

"Why?"

"For the money."

He dug around in the ground with a finger, picked up a pebble and added: "Who's going to pay for it? That's all that interests my uncle. Your parents have said that they'll take care of everything. Board and lodging, school, the lot. For him it's a real bargain."

"And what does your aunt say about it?"

"It's fine by her."

"And your mother?"

Bruno snorted. He threw the pebble into the water. It was so small that it made no sound. "What my mother always says. The usual. A big nothing."

There was a layer of dried mud on the rocks on the bank. A black crust showing the level the lake had reached in spring. Now the snowfields that fed it had been reduced to gray stains in the gullies, and if the summer were to continue it would end up by making them disappear altogether. Without the snow, who knows what would happen to the lake.

"And what about you?" I asked.

"What about me?"

"Would you like to?"

"To come to Milan?" said Bruno. "I haven't a clue. Do you know that ever since yesterday I've been trying to imagine what it would be like? And I can't do it. I have no idea what it would be like."

We remained in silence. I, who knew only too well what it was like, did not have to imagine anything in order to be opposed to the idea. Bruno would have hated Milan, and Milan would have ruined Bruno, just like when his aunt washed and dressed him up and sent him around to us to conjugate verbs. I really could not understand why my parents were going out of their way to turn him into something that he wasn't. What was wrong with letting him graze cows for the rest of his life? I was unaware of the selfishness of this thought, that it wasn't really concerned with Bruno, with his own wishes and his future—but only with the use I could continue to make of him. I was thinking of my summers, my companion, my own experience of the mountain. I hoped that, up there, nothing would ever change—not even the charred shacks or mounds of manure lining the road—that he should stay the same, always, along with the piles of manure and the ruins, frozen in time and awaiting my arrival.

"Well, maybe you should tell them," I suggested.

"Tell them what?"

"That you don't want to go to Milan. That you want to stay here."

Bruno turned to look at me. He raised his eyebrows. He had not expected such advice from me. Although he may have been thinking the very same thing himself, coming from me it did not seem right. "Are you crazy?" he said. "I'm not staying here. I've spent my whole life going up and down this mountain."

Then he got to his feet, and there on the grass where we stood he cupped his hands round his mouth and shouted, "Oh! Can you hear me? It's me, Bruno! I'm leaving!"

From the other side of the lake the slope of the Grenon sent back to us an echo of his cry. We heard some stones falling. His shout had startled a group of chamois that was now clambering up the scree.

It was Bruno who pointed them out to me. They were passing through rocks which made them almost invisible, but when they crossed a snowfield I was able to count them. It was a small herd of five. They climbed up that stain of snow in single file, reached the crest, and lingered there for a moment, as if to look at us for one last time before going. Then, one by one, they disappeared down the other side.

• • •

Our four-thousander that summer was meant to be the Castor. We would scale one of these each year, my father and I, on the Monte Rosa, so as to conclude the season on a high, when we were best trained up to do so. I hadn't stopped going onto the glacier, but neither had I stopped suffering its effects: I had just become accustomed to feeling unwell and to the fact that this sickness formed a normal part of that world, like getting up before dawn, or the freeze-dried food in the refuges, or the cawing of crows on the heights. It was a way of going into the mountains that for me had lost all sense of adventure. It was a brutal putting of one foot after the other before vomiting my heart out at the top. I hated doing it, and found myself hating that white desert every time: and yet I was proud of going above four thousand meters again, as further proof of my courage. In 1985 my father's black felt-tip ink had reached the Vincent, by 1986 the Gnifetti. He considered the ascent of these summits to be a kind of training for me. He had consulted a doctor and was convinced that I would grow out of my altitude sickness, so that over the course of three or four years we would reach the point when we could do more serious things, such as crossing the Lyskamm or the rock faces of Dufour.

But what I remember most about Castor, even more than its elongated crests, was the vigil that we shared in the refuge. A plate of pasta, a half-liter of wine on the table, the mountaineers nearby arguing amongst themselves, ruddy-faced from the sun and from fatigue. The prospect of the next day created in the room a kind of concentration. In front of me my father was leafing through the guest book, his favorite reading in a refuge. He spoke German well and understood French, and every so often he would translate a passage from these languages of the Alps. Someone had returned to a summit after thirty years and thanked God. Someone else regretted the absence of a friend. He was moved by these things, to the point where he took up the pen to make his own contribution to that collective diary.

When he got up to refill his carafe I looked at what he had written. His handwriting was dense and nervous, difficult to decipher if you were not already familiar with it. I read: *I'm here with my fourteen-year-old son, Pietro. These will be my last occasions at the head of the rope, because soon he will be the one pulling me up. Don't much feel like going back to the city, but I'll take with me the memory of these days as the most beautiful refuge.* It was signed: Giovanni Guasti.

Rather than making me feel moved, or proud, these words just annoyed me. I detected in them something that sounded false and sentimental, a rhetoric of the mountains that did not correspond to reality. If it was such a paradise then why did we not stay and live up there? Why were we taking away a friend who had been born and raised there? And if the city was so revolting, why were we forcing him to live in it with us? This is what I would like to have asked my father—and my mother as well, come to think of it. How is it that you are so sure of knowing what's best for the course of another person's life? How is it that you don't have the slightest doubt—that he might know better than you?

But when my father returned he was in high spirits. It was the third from last day of his holiday, a Friday in August of his forty-sixth year, and he was in an Alpine refuge with his only son. He had brought another glass and half-filled it for me. Perhaps, in his imagination, now that I was growing up and getting over my altitude sickness, our relationship as father and son would be transformed into something different. Climbing companions, just like he had written in the book. Drinking companions. Perhaps he really did imagine us like this in a few years' time, sitting at a table at three and a half thousand meters drinking red wine and studying maps of the routes, with no more secrets between us.

"How's your stomach doing?" he asked.

"It's not bad."

"And your legs?"

"They're really good."

"Excellent. Tomorrow we'll have fun."

My father raised his glass. I did the same, tasted the wine and felt that I liked it. While I was getting it down a guy sitting nearby burst out laughing, said something in German, and clapped me hard on the back, as if I had just been initiated into the great brotherhood of men and he was welcoming me into it.

• • •

The next evening we went back to Grana as veterans of the glacier. My father with his shirt unbuttoned and his rucksack slung over one shoulder, and with a hobbling gait due to the blisters on his feet; I as ravenous as a wolf, since as soon as we descended from altitude my stomach realized that it had been empty for two days. My mother was waiting for us with a hot bath and supper already on the table. Later on the time for telling our story would come: my father tried to describe the color of ice in the crevasses, the vertiginous nature of the north faces, the elegance of the cornices of snow on the crests; while I for my part had only blurred recollections of such visions, fogged as they were by nausea. I usually kept quiet. I had already learned a fact which my father never resigned himself to, namely, that it was impossible to convey what it feels like up there to those who have stayed below.

But that evening we did not get around to telling my mother anything. I was about to have my bath when I heard the voice of a man ranting down in the courtyard. I went to the window and pulled back the curtain: I saw a character who was gesticulating and yelling words that I could not understand. My father was the only other one out there. He had hung his thick socks on the balcony and was bathing his aching feet in the trough, getting up from where he sat on its rim to confront the stranger.

For a moment I thought it might be a farmer furious at this misuse of his water. In Grana they would leap at any pretext to take offense from an incomer. It was easy to identify the locals: they all moved in the same way, had the same marked facial features from out of which, between cheekbones and forehead, a pair of sky-blue eyes peered. This man was smaller than my father, except for the muscular arms and huge hands that were completely out of proportion to the rest of his body. With those hands he grabbed the two sides of my father's shirt just below the collar. It looked as if he wanted to pick him up.

My father spread his arms. I was seeing him from behind and imagined that he would be saying: calm down, calm down. The man mumbled something, showing his ruined teeth. His face was also wrecked: I didn't know by what, being still too young to recognize the face of a drinker. He made a grimace that was exactly like one of Luigi Guglielmina's, and at that moment I realized how much he resembled him. My father began to gesture slowly. I understood that he was explaining something, and knowing him, knew also that his arguments would be unanswerable. The man lowered his gaze, just as I always did. It looked as if he was having second thoughts, but he kept hold of my father's shirt. My father turned up the palms of his hands as if to say: OK, do we understand each other? So now what? There was something ridiculous in seeing him in this situation barefoot. On his calves the line made by his socks sharply divided his pale ankles from a narrow band of scarlet skin just below the knee—the area that his plus fours left bare. Here was the educated city-dweller, sure of himself and used to telling others what to do, who had just burned his legs on the glacier and was now trying to reason with a highlander the worse for drink.

The man decided that he'd had enough. Suddenly and without warning, he lowered his right hand to make a fist and hit my father on the temple. It was the first time in my life that I had seen a real punch thrown. The sound of knuckle on cheekbone was clear even from the bathroom, dry as a whack with a stick. My father took two steps back, staggered, but managed not to fall. But immediately afterwards his arms fell to his sides and his shoulders sagged a little. It was the posture of a wretched man. The other man said something else before leaving, a threat or a promise, and it did not surprise me to see him heading, in the end, towards the Guglielminas' house. During that brief confrontation I had realized who he was.

He had come back to reclaim what was his. He did not know that he had got the wrong person. But in the end it made no difference: that blow was thrown into my father's face in order to plant something clearly in the mind of my mother. It was the eruption of reality into her idealism, and perhaps also into her arrogance. The next day Bruno and his father were nowhere to be seen. My father's left eye became swollen and blue. But I don't think that was what was hurting most, when he got into his car that evening and left for Milan.

The following week was our last in Grana. Bruno's aunt came to speak to my mother: mortified, wary, worried, perhaps above all by the prospect of losing such faithful tenants. My mother reassured her. She was already thinking about damage limitation, about how to salvage the relationships that had been so painstakingly nurtured.

For me it proved to be an interminable week. It rained constantly: a blanket of low-lying cloud cover hid the mountains from view, occasionally clearing to expose the first snow at three thousand meters. I would like to have taken one of the paths I knew and gone up to tread all over it, without asking permission from anyone. But I stayed in the village instead, replaying what I had seen and feeling guilty about what had happened. Then on Sunday we locked the house and left as well.

FOUR

I COULD NOT GET that blow out of my mind until a few years later I found the courage to deliver one myself. In truth it was the first of a series, and the hardest of these I would go on to land in the valley in later years, but now it seems right that my rebellion should have begun in the mountains, like everything else that has mattered to me. The event itself was unremarkable. I was sixteen and one day my father decided to take me camping. He had bought an old heavy tent from a stall selling army surplus gear. He had this idea of putting it up on the side of a small lake, fishing for a few trout without being discovered by the forest rangers, lighting a fire at nightfall and roasting the fish on it—and afterwards, who knows, staying up late drinking and singing, warmed by its embers.

He had never shown the slightest interest in camping, so I suspected that there was something else that had been planned for me. In recent times I had withdrawn into a corner from which I observed our family life with a pitiless eye. The ineradicably fixed habits of my parents, my father's harmless outbursts of anger and the tricks that my mother used to contain them, the little bullyings and the subterfuges that they no longer realized they were resorting to. He would be emotional, authoritarian, irascible; she would be strong and calm and conciliatory. They had a mutually reassuring way of always playing the same part, knowing that the other would play theirs: these were not real arguments; they were performances with always predictable endings, and in that cage I also ended up being caught. I had begun to feel an urgent need to escape. But I had never managed to say so: not once had I uttered a single protest about anything, and I think that it was precisely for this, to make me *speak*, that the damn tent had materialized.

After lunch my father spread out the equipment in the kitchen and divided it up so as to distribute its weight equally between us. The poles and pegs alone must have weighed ten kilos. With the sleeping bags, anoraks, sweaters, and food supplies on top, the rucksacks soon became full. With one knee on the kitchen floor my father began to loosen every strap and then to push, compress, pull—at war with mass and volume, and I could already feel myself sweating beneath that load in the sweltering afternoon heat. But it wasn't only the weight that was unbearable. It was the scene that he had conjured up, or that they had: the campfire, the lake, the trout, the starry sky; all that intimacy.

"Dad," I said. "Come on, that's enough."

"Wait, wait," he said, still trying to stuff something inside the rucksack, absorbed by the effort.

"No, I mean it: it's no good."

My father stopped what he was doing and looked up. He had a furious expression on his face from his exertions, and the way he looked at me made me feel like another hostile rucksack, another strap that wouldn't comply.

I shrugged.

With my father, if I kept quiet it meant that he could speak. He unfurrowed his brow and said: "Well, perhaps we can take some stuff out. Lend a hand if you feel like it."

"No," I replied. "I really don't feel like doing this."

"What don't you feel like doing, the camping?"

"The tent, the lake, the whole thing."

"What do you mean *the whole thing*?"

"I don't want it. I'm not coming."

I could not have dealt him a harder blow. Refusing to follow him into the mountains: it was inevitable that it would happen sooner or later, he must have expected it. But sometimes I think that because he had no father of his own he had no experience of making certain kinds of attack, and was therefore ill-prepared to receive one. He was deeply hurt. Maybe he could have asked me a few more questions, and it would have been a good occasion to hear what I had to say—but in the event he wasn't capable of doing so, or didn't think it was necessary, or at that moment he just felt too offended to think. He left the rucksacks, the tent, and the sleeping bags where they were and went out for a walk by himself. For me it was a liberation.

• • •

Bruno had been dealt the opposite fate, and was now working with his father as a builder. I hardly ever saw him. They worked high up in the mountains building refuges and *alpeggi*, and slept up there on weekdays. I would encounter him on a Friday or Saturday, not in Grana but in some cafe bar down in the valley. I had all the time that I wanted now that I had freed myself from the obligation to climb mountains, and while my father scaled the summits I would head in the opposite direction, searching for someone my own age. It only took two or three attempts before I was admitted into the company of holidaymakers: I spent the afternoons between the benches of a tennis court and the tables of a cafe bar, hoping that no one would notice that I had no money with which to order anything. I listened to the chat, watched the girls, every so often looked up at the mountains. I recognized the pastures and the minuscule white stains that were plastered huts. The bright green of the larches that gave way to the more sombre green of the firs, the "right" side in sunlight and the "reverse" in shadow. I knew that I had little enough in common, and to share, with those young people on their holidays, but I wanted to fight against my inclination towards solitude—to try to be with others for a while and to see what might happen.

Later, towards seven, the workmen would arrive at the bar: the bricklayers, the cattle breeders. They would get out of white vans and 4x4s, filthy with mud or lime or sawdust, moving with a lolling gait that they had learned in adolescence, as if together with the weight of their own bodies they were always moving another, greater one. They would take up positions at the counter, complaining and cursing, bantering with the waitresses and ordering rounds of drinks. Bruno was with them. I could see that he had developed his muscles, and that he liked to show them off by rolling his shirtsleeves high. He owned a collection of caps and a wallet that stuck out from the back pocket of his jeans. This struck me more than anything else, given that for me, earning money was still a distant prospect. He would spend it without even counting, paying for his round with some crumpled banknote or other, imitating the others.

But then at a certain point, with the same distracted air, he would turn towards me from the counter. He knew already that he would meet my gaze. He would give a signal with his chin, and I would reply by raising the fingers of one hand. We looked at each other for a second. That was it. No one noticed; it wasn't repeated during the course of the evening; and I wasn't sure if I was interpreting properly the significance of this greeting. It could mean: I remember you, I miss you. Or it might be: it's only been two years but it seems like a lifetime, doesn't it? Or perhaps: hey Berio, what are you doing with that crowd? I didn't know what Bruno thought about the clash between our fathers. Whether he had any regrets about how things had turned out, or if seen from his current point of view that whole story seemed as distant and as unreal as it did to me. He didn't have the look of someone who was unhappy at all. On the other hand it could be that I did.

His father was with him in the row of drinkers, amongst those with the more irritating voices and the always-empty glasses. He treated Bruno as if he was just another of his drinking companions. I disliked this man, but envied him in one respect: there was nothing perceptible between them, not a more brusque or solicitous tone of voice, not a gesture of irritation, confidence, or embarrassment—and if you did not know it already there was nothing to indicate that they were father and son.

• • •

Not all of the young men of the valley wasted their summer in the bar. After a few days someone took me to a place on the other side of the river, a wood of wild pines which concealed some huge monoliths, as alien to that landscape as meteorites. The glacier must have pushed them to that point in some far distant past. Then the earth and the leaves and the moss had covered them, pines had grown around and on top of them—but some of these stones had been brought back to light, cleaned up with wire brushes, and even christened with individual names. The youths would challenge each other to find every possible way of climbing them. Without ropes or pegs they tried and retried approaches from about a meter above ground level, ending up by landing softly in the undergrowth. It was a pleasure to watch the two or three strongest: agile as gymnasts, with hands scoured and white with chalk, they had brought this pastime to the mountain from the city. They were happy enough to teach it to others and I asked them if I could have a go. After all, I had already climbed with Bruno every kind of rock without knowing anything, since my father had always warned me against adventuring any place where you were dependent on using your hands. And perhaps it was because of this that I decided to become good at it.

At sunset the group expanded to include those who had come

to party. Someone would light a fire, someone else would bring something to smoke and something to drink. Then we would sit around, and while the bottle of wine circulated I would listen to discussions about things that were completely new to me and that fascinated me every bit as much as the girls sitting on the other side of the fire. I heard about the Californian hippies who had invented modern free-form climbing, bivouacking for entire summers beneath the rock faces of the Yosemite and climbing half-naked; or about the French climbers who trained on the sea cliffs of Provence, wore their hair long, and were accustomed to going up swiftly and light-footed—how when they moved from the sea to the gullies of Mont Blanc they would humiliate veteran climbers such as my father. Rock climbing was all about the pleasure of being together, about being free to experiment, and for this a two-meter-high stone on the bank of a river was as good as any at eight thousand meters: it had nothing whatsoever to do with the cult of difficulty, or with the conquest of summits. I listened while the woods became shrouded in darkness. The twisted trunks of the pines, the powerful fragrance of resin, the white monoliths in the light of the fire made it a more welcoming refuge than any of those on Monte Rosa. Later on somebody would begin to try a route with a cigarette between his lips, his sense of balance skewed by drink; someone else would wander off with a girl at his side.

The differences between us counted for less in the woods, perhaps because they were less evident there than elsewhere. They were wealthy young men from Milan, Genoa, and Turin. The less well-off lived in small villas high up in the valley, buildings erected in crazy haste at the foot of the ski slopes; the richest in the old-style mountain dwellings in exclusive areas, where each stone and every slate had been removed, numbered, and then placed back according to the design of an architect. I happened to go into one of these accompanying a friend who was fetching drink for the evening. From outside it looked like an old timber-built barn; inside it revealed itself to be the house of an antiques dealer, or a collector: virtually an exhibition of fine-art books, paintings, furniture, sculpture. And of bottles as well: my friend opened a cupboard and we each filled a rucksack.

"But won't your father be angry that we're pinching his wine?" I asked.

"My father!" he replied, as if he found the very word ridiculous. We emptied the cellar and ran for the woods.

• • •

In the meantime my own father was mortally offended. He had begun to go to the mountains again, alone, getting up at dawn and leaving before we were awake, and sometimes during his absence I would take a look at his map in order to check on his latest conquests. He had started to explore a part of the valley that we had always avoided, since you could tell from below that there was nothing up there: neither villages, nor water, nor refuges, nor stunning peaks—only bare slopes that climbed steeply for two thousand meters, and an endless expanse of scree. I think he went there to cool down his disappointment, or to find a landscape that resembled his state of mind. He never again invited me to join him. From his perspective I had become the one who needed to go to him: if I was the one who'd had the courage to say *no*, then the onus was on me now to say *sorry* and *please.*

The time of the glacier came round again, our two days of glory in the mid-August holiday, and I saw him preparing the crampons, the pickaxe as severe as a weapon, the water bottle dented by all the knocks it had taken. He seemed to me like the last survivor of one of those Alpine expeditions, one of those soldier-climbers who went in the thirties to die in droves on the north faces of the Alps, blindly attacking the mountain.

"You need to speak to him," my mother said that morning. "Look how hurt he is."

"But shouldn't he be the one speaking to me?"

"You're capable of doing it; he isn't."

"But capable of doing what?"

"Come on, you know full well. He's only waiting for you to go and ask to come with him."

I did know it—but I did not do it. I went to my room, and shortly afterwards watched from the window as my father walked off with a heavy tread, his rucksack stuffed with metal gear. You don't go up the glacier on your own, and I knew that in the evening he would have to resort to a humiliating search. There was always at least one person in his predicament in the refuge: he would go from table to table, he would listen to the discussions for a while, joining the conversation, and would eventually propose joining the group the next morning, despite knowing that nobody was keen to tie a stranger to his rope. At that moment it seemed to me like the perfect punishment for him.

• • •

I tasted my own punishment too, that summer. After much training on the monoliths, I went with two youths on my first real free-form climb. One of them was the wine thief, the son of the collector, a Genoese who was amongst the strongest in the group; the other was a friend of his who had started a few months ago, probably just to be with him, since he had not much passion, dedication, or talent for climbing. The rock face was so close to the road that we only had to cross a meadow to reach the point of attack, an overhang jutting out so far that the cattle used it to shelter from the wind and rain. We put our shoes on amongst the cows, then the Genoese handed me a harness and a locking carabiner and tied the two of us to the ends of the rope with himself in the middle. Without further ceremony he told the other boy to go safely and we set off.

He climbed lightly and flexibly, giving the impression of being weightless, and that his every movement was effortless. He did not need to feel around to find the right point of purchase, but just hit the mark every time. Every so often he unhooked a quickdraw from the harness, clipped it onto one of the bolts that marked the way, and would pass the rope through the carabiner; then he would plunge his hands into the bag of chalk, blow on his fingers, and start to climb again with ease. He looked very elegant. Elegance, grace, lightness, they were all qualities that I was so keen to learn from him.

His friend had no such qualities. I could see him close up, climbing, because when the Genoese arrived at the resting place he shouted down to us to climb up together, leaving just a few meters' distance between us. And so, one pull after another, I found myself with his companion directly above my head. I had frequently to stop because my head was right beneath his shoes, at which point I would turn round to look at the world behind my shoulders: the fields yellowed at the end of August, the river sparkling in the sunlight, cars already miniaturized on the trunk road. The drop did not frighten me. Away from the ground, in the air, I felt good and the movements of the climb came naturally to my body, requiring concentration but not exceptional muscles or lungs.

My companion instead used his arms too much and his feet not enough. He clung close to the rock so was obliged to seek handholds blind, and he did not refrain from grabbing hold of a bolt when he found no alternative.

"You shouldn't do it like that," I told him, making a big mistake. I should have let him do it in whichever way he thought best.

He looked at me, annoyed, and said: "What do you want? Are you trying to overtake? You're always pressing from down there."

From that moment I had made an enemy. At the resting place he said to the other one, "Pietro's in a hurry, he thinks it's a race."

I didn't say: your friend is a cheat who hangs on the bolts. I understood that it would have ended up two against one. I kept my distance from then on, but the guy would not let it go: every so often he would make a crack at my expense, and my competitiveness became a running joke for the rest of the day. According to that joke I was running behind them, I would get to just below them and they would have to give me a few kicks to get me out from under their feet. The collector's son laughed. When I reached the last resting place he said: "You're going strong. Do you want to try going first?"

"Fine," I answered. In reality I wanted to get it over with as soon as possible, so that they would leave me in peace. I already had my safety harness and all the clips; we didn't have to make any of the usual maneuvers required to exchange places—so I looked up, saw a bolt planted in a fissure, and set off.

Finding your way is easy if you have a rope above your head: it's something else entirely when the rope is at your feet. The bolt on which I hooked the first clip was an old ring nail, not one of the steel bolts that glinted along the rock face. I decided to ignore the fact and to advance along the fissure, as I was already making good progress. The thing was, though, that further up the crack began to narrow and soon disappeared altogether. I now had jutting out above me a black, damp roof of rock—and no idea as to how to get over it.

"Where do I go?" I shouted.

"I can't see from here," the Genoese shouted back. "Are there any bolts there?"

No, there were no bolts. I held fast to the last bit of the fissure, and leaned out first to one side of it and then the other, to see if I could spot any. I discovered that I had followed a false trail: the line of steel plaquettes ran up at a diagonal a few meters to my right, skirting the overhang and reaching to the top.

"I've taken the wrong route!" I shouted.

"Oh, really?" he shouted back in response. "And what's it like there? Can you get over it?"

"No. It's completely smooth."

"Then you'll have to come back down." I couldn't see them, but could hear that they were amused.

I had never climbed backwards. The fissure that I had come up looked impossible when seen from above. I felt an impulse to hold on even more tightly, and at the same time realized that the rusty iron peg was now some four or five meters away. One of my legs began to tremble: an uncontrollable trembling that began at the knee and went down to my heel. My foot no longer responded. My hands were sweating, and the rock seemed to be slipping from my grasp.

"I'm falling," I shouted. "Hold tight!"

Then I went down. A fall of ten meters is not really anything very serious, but you need to know *how* to fall: push yourself away from the rock face and cushion the impact with your feet. No one had taught me how to do this and I went straight down, flaying myself on the rock in my attempt to get a grip on it. I felt a tightness in my groin when I reached the bottom. Yet this other pain was fortunate—it meant that someone had blocked the rope. Now they were not laughing anymore.

Shortly afterwards we came out on the top of the rock, and it felt strange at that point to find ourselves in the fields again, with a taut line a step from the precipice, the cows grazing, a half-derelict farmstead, a dog barking. I was shaken and in pain, I had blood everywhere, and I suspect that the two friends felt guilty, since one of them asked me: "Are you sure you're all right?"

"Sure."

"Do you want a cigarette?"

"Thanks."

I decided that it would be the last thing we would ever share. I smoked it lying on the grass, looking up at the sky. They said something else to me, but by that stage I wasn't listening anymore.

Just as it did every summer the weather changed at the end of the month. It started raining and getting cold, and it was the mountain itself that prompted in you the desire to go down to the valley to enjoy the warmth of September. My father had left again. My mother began to light the stove: in brief breaks in the weather I would go into the woods to collect firewood, bending down the dry branches of larches until they broke with a sharp crack. I felt fine up there in Grana, but this time I too was anxious to return to the city. I felt that I had so many things to discover, people to go in search of, and that the near future held important changes in store for me. I lived those last days knowing that they were the last in more than one sense, as if they were memories of the mountain that were already in the past. I liked the fact that we were like this: my mother and I alone together again, the fire crackling in the kitchen, the cold of the early morning, the hours spent reading and wandering in the woods. There were no rocks to climb in Grana, but I discovered that I could train well enough by climbing the walls of derelict houses. I would go up and come down the corners methodically, avoiding the easiest handholds and trying to support myself using only the cracks and the tips of my fingers. Then I would cross from one corner to another and back. In this way I must have climbed every derelict building in the village.

One Sunday the sky was clear again. We were having breakfast when there was a knock at the door. It was Bruno. He was standing there on the balcony, smiling.

"Hey, Berio," he said. "Coming into the mountains?"

Without any preamble he explained to me that his uncle had had the idea of acquiring some goats that summer. He would leave them to graze freely on the mountain near the *alpeggio*, so that he needed to do nothing except check on them through binoculars in the evening, making sure that they were all there and had not strayed from where he could keep an eye on them. The problem was that during their first few nights up there it had snowed, and now his uncle couldn't find them. Chances were that they had sought shelter in some hole or other, or run off behind a passing herd of ibexes. Bruno spoke of it as if it was just one more example of his uncle's harebrained schemes.

He owned a motorbike now, an old rusted one without number plates, and with this we took the road leading up to the farmstead, dodging the lowest branches of the larches and getting covered in mud going through puddles. I liked gripping his back riding pillion, and sensed no embarrassment on his part. On the other side of his uncle's meadows we took a straight track at a good speed: in this patchy and stony grass the goats' droppings were everywhere. Following them, we climbed up a bank of rhododendrons and of fallen rock where a nearly dry river ran. Then the snow began.

Up to that moment I had known only one of the mountains' seasons: a short-lived summer that resembled spring at the beginning of July, and autumn at the end of August. About winter I knew next to nothing. Bruno and I used to speak about it often enough as children, when my return to the city was approaching and I became melancholy and imagined what it would be like to live up there with him all the year round.

"But you don't know what it's like up here in the winter," he would say. "There's nothing but snow."

"I'd love to see it," I would reply.

And now here it was. This wasn't the frozen snow of the gorges at three thousand meters: it was fresh soft snow that got into your shoes and soaked your feet, and it was strange to lift them and to see, compressed in your footprint, the wildflowers of August. The snow barely reached to my ankles, but it was deep enough to have covered all traces of the track. It covered the bushes, the holes and stones, so that every step was a potential trap, and with my lack of experience walking on such snow I could only follow Bruno by stepping into his footprints. As when we were younger, I could not understand by what memory or instinct he was guided. I just followed.

We reached the ridge that overlooked the other side, and as soon as the wind turned it carried to us the sound of bells. The goats had taken shelter lower down, beneath the first rocks. Reaching them was simple enough: they were huddling in groups of three or four, the mothers with their kids around them, in clearings in the snow. Counting them Bruno saw that there was not a single one missing. They were less obedient than cattle, some feral after a summer spent on the mountain, and climbing back over our own tracks he had to shout to keep them together, throwing snowballs at any that strayed and cursing his uncle and his brilliant ideas. Eventually we reached the crest again, and went down onto the snow in unruly and noisy procession.

It must have been midday by the time we had the grass beneath our feet. Suddenly it was summer again. The goats, famished, scattered over the meadow. For our part we began to rush down, not because we were in any particular hurry but because this was the only way we knew of being in the mountains, and the descent had always exhilarated us.

When we reached the motorbike Bruno said: "I saw you while you were rock climbing. You're good."

"I started this summer."

"And do you like it?"

"A lot."

"As much as the river game?"

I laughed. "No," I said. "Not that much."

"This summer I've built a wall."

"Where?"

"Up in the mountains, in a stable. It was falling down and we had to rebuild it completely. The problem was, there was no road, and I went back and forth on the bike. We had to work like in the old times: spade, bucket, and pickaxe."

"And do you enjoy it?"

"Yes," he said, after mulling it over a bit. "The work, yes. It's difficult to build a wall in that way."

There was something else that he didn't like, but he didn't tell me what and I didn't ask him. I didn't ask him how he was getting on with his father, or how much money he was earning, or if he had a girlfriend or any plans for the future, or about what he thought of what had happened between us. Nor did he ask me anything. He didn't ask how I was, or how my parents were, and I didn't reply: my mother's well, my father's still fucked off with me. That things had changed a bit that summer. I thought that I had found some friends, but I was mistaken. I had kissed two girls in one evening.

Instead I just told him that I would go back to Grana on foot.

"Are you sure?"

"Yes, I'm leaving tomorrow and I feel like walking."

"Right. Be seeing you then."

It was my end of summer ritual: a last wander around alone to say goodbye to the mountains. I watched as Bruno straddled the motorcycle and started it after a few attempts, with a puff of black smoke from the exhaust. He had a certain style as a motorcyclist. He raised a hand in farewell and revved the engine. I returned his wave, even though he was no longer looking at me.

I had no way of knowing it then, but we would not meet up again for a very long time. The next year I turned seventeen and would only return to Grana for a few days, and would then stop going there altogether. The future would take me away from this mountain of my childhood; it was a sad, a beautiful, and an inevitable fact that I had already become fully aware of. When Bruno and his motorcycle disappeared into the wood I turned towards the slope we had come down, staying there a while before leaving, looking at the long line of our tracks in the snow.

TWO

The House of Reconciliation

FIVE

MY FATHER DIED when he was sixty-two and I was thirty-one. It was only at his funeral that I realized I was the same age now as he'd been when I was born. But my thirty-one years had little enough in common with his: I had not married; I had not gone to work in a factory; I had not fathered a son; and my life seemed to me to be only partly that of a grown man, and partly still like that of an adolescent. I lived alone in a studio flat, a luxury which I struggled to afford. I would like to have made a living as a documentary filmmaker, but to pay the rent I accepted work of every kind. I too had emigrated: having inherited from my parents the idea that at a key point in one's youth it was necessary to leave the place where you'd been born and raised in order to go and develop elsewhere, I had at twenty-three, and fresh out of military service, left Milan to join a girlfriend in Turin. My relationship with the girl did not last, but my relationship with the city did. Between its ancient rivers and in its arcade cafes I'd felt immediately at home. I was reading Hemingway, and wandered around penniless, trying to keep myself open to new encounters, to offers of work and to every possibility, with the mountains as the background to my moveable feast: even if I had never gone back there, to glimpse sight of them on my horizon every time I left the apartment seemed like a blessing.

And so it was that a hundred and twenty kilometers of rice fields now divided me from my father. It was no distance, but to cover it you had to want to do so. A couple of years previously I had given him one last great disappointment by abandoning my university studies: I had always excelled at maths, and he had always foreseen for me a future similar to his own. My father told me that I was throwing my life away; I replied that he had thrown away his before me. We didn't speak for an entire year after that, during which time I was coming and going between home and my military barracks, returning from leave with scarcely a word in parting. It was better for both of us that I should follow my own path, invent a life different from his in some other place—and once that distance was established, neither of us was inclined to close it.

With my mother it was different. Since I was not one to speak much on the phone she took it upon herself to write me letters. She discovered soon enough that I would reply. I liked to sit down at the table of an evening, take pen and paper, and tell her what was happening with me. It was by letter that I told her of my decision to enroll in a film school. It was there that I made my first friends in Turin. I was fascinated by documentary film and felt that I had a vocation for observing and listening, so it was good to get her reassurance: *Yes, you've always been good at that.* I knew that it would take a long time to turn it into a profession, but she encouraged me from the outset. For years she would send me money, and I would send her in return everything that I was making: portraits of people and places, explorations of the city—short films that nobody ever saw but of which I was proud. I liked the life that was taking shape around me. This is what I would tell her when she asked if I was happy. I avoided answering her other questions—about the relationships with girlfriends, which never lasted more than a few months, since as soon as they became serious I would extricate myself from them.

And you? I would write.

I'm fine, my mother would answer, *but your dad is working too hard, and it's damaging his health.* She would tell me more about him than about herself. The factory was in financial crisis and my father, after a thirty-year career, was redoubling his efforts instead of slowing down and biding his time before retirement. He was spending a lot of time in the car alone, driving hundreds of kilometers between one plant and another, returning home exhausted and collapsing into bed immediately after supper. His sleep was short-lived: at night he would get up and go back to work, unable to rest because of his worries, which according to my mother were not only about the factory. *He's always been anxious, but now it's becoming an illness.* He was anxious about his work, anxious about approaching old age, anxious because my mother had flu—and he was anxious about me as well. He would be jolted awake with the thought that I was unwell. So he would ask her to phone me, even if it meant getting me out of bed; she was unable to convince him to wait a few hours but tried to calm him, to get him back to sleep, to slow him down. It was not as if his own body hadn't been giving him signs that he should do so, but he only knew how to live this way, with everything breathing down his neck: imploring him to calm down was like constraining him to go up a mountain *more slowly,* to avoid getting into a race with anyone, to enjoy the health-giving properties of the air.

He was only partly the man that I knew, and partly another—the one that I was discovering through my mother's letters. I was intrigued by this other side to him. It brought to mind a certain fragility that I had only glimpsed before, certain moments of confusion which he would immediately attempt to conceal. When I would lean out over a rock and he would instinctively make a grab for my trouser belt. When I was sick on the glacier and he would be more worried about it than I was myself. It occurred to me that perhaps this other father had always been there at my side, and that I had failed to notice him, however difficult the first one was; and I began to think that in the future I should—or could—make an attempt to build bridges with him.

Then that future vanished in an instant, together with the possibilities it contained. One March evening in 2004 my mother called to tell me that my father had suffered a heart attack on the motorway. They had found him in a lay-by. He had not caused an accident; in fact he had managed to do everything correctly: he had stopped at the side of the road and put on the hazard lights, as if he had a flat tire or had run out of petrol. Instead it was his heart that had completely failed on him. Too many miles on the clock, too little maintenance: my father must have felt an acute pain in his chest and had enough time to realize what was happening. In the lay-by he had turned off the engine. But he hadn't even unbuckled his seat belt. He had stayed sitting there, and that's how they found him—like a racing driver who had retired from the race, the most ironic way for someone like him to go, with his hands still on the wheel, being overtaken by everyone else.

• • •

That spring I went back to Milan for a few weeks to be with my mother. Apart from the practicalities that needed to be dealt with, I felt the need to be with her for a while. After the turbulent days of the funeral, in the calm that followed, we discovered to my surprise that my father had thought thoroughly about his own death. In his desk drawer there was a list of instructions, attached to which were details of his bank accounts, and everything else that was required for us to inherit his assets. Since we were the only inheritors, he had not been obliged by Italian law to make a formal will. But on the same piece of paper on which he had specified that he left to my mother his half of the apartment in Milan, for me there was the phrase *I would like Pietro to have*—followed mysteriously by *the property in Grana*. No last words, not a line of farewell or explanation: it was all cold and practical and legalistic.

About this inheritance my mother knew next to nothing. There is a tendency to assume that one's parents share everything that crosses their minds, especially as they get older, but I was discovering in those days that after my departure they had led more or less separate lives. He worked and was always traveling. Having retired from her own job, she was doing voluntary work as a nurse in a clinic for immigrants, helping with prenatal classes—and spent most of her other time with friends rather than with my father. She knew only that he had acquired the previous year, and for not much money, a small piece of land in the mountains. He had not sought her permission to spend the money, or even invited her to see the place—it was a long time since they had gone out walking together—and she had not objected, considering it to be some altogether private concern.

Amongst my father's papers I found the contract of the purchase and the land registry document, neither of which enlightened me much further. I had inherited an agricultural building four meters by seven at the center of an irregular plot of land. The map was too small to work out where this place was, and too different from the ones I was used to: it did not show the altitude or the paths, only the property, and looking at it told you nothing about whether it was surrounded by woods, fields, or by anything else for that matter.

My mother said: "Bruno will know where it is."

"Bruno?"

"They were always going off together."

"I didn't know that they'd even seen each other again."

"Of course, we both saw him again. It's quite difficult not to meet up in a place like Grana, wouldn't you say?"

"What's he doing now?" I asked, though what I really wanted to ask was: "How is he? Does he remember me? During all these years had he thought about me as much as I thought about him?" But I had learned by now to ask questions in the adult way, asking one thing in order to find out about another.

"He's a bricklayer."

"So he never moved away?"

"Bruno? And where do you think he would go? Things have not changed much in Grana, you'll see."

• • •

I did not know whether to believe her, since I had certainly changed a lot in the meantime. As an adult, a place that you loved as a young boy might appear entirely different to you, and turn out to be a disappointment; or it might remind you of what you once were but no longer are, becoming a cause for great sadness. I wasn't that keen to find out how it would be. But there was this property that I had been left, and curiosity got the better of me: I went there at the end of April, alone, in my father's car. It was evening, and climbing up the valley I could only see the areas illuminated by the lights. Even so I noticed several changes: the points at which the road had been improved and widened, the protective netting over the escarpments, the piles of felled tree trunks. Someone had started to build little villas in a Tyrolese style, while someone else had started to extract sand and gravel from the river, which was shored up now between cement banks, where it had once flowed between stones and trees. The second homes in darkness, the hotels closed out of season or shut for good, the immobile bulldozers and the excavators with their arms stuck in the ground gave the landscape an air of industrial decline, like those building sites left semi-abandoned due to bankruptcy.

Then just as I was letting myself feel depressed by these discoveries, something called out for my attention, and I leaned over towards the windscreen to look up. In the night sky some white shapes emitted a kind of aura. It took me a moment to realize that they were not clouds: they were mountains still covered in snow. I should have expected it, in April. But in the city the spring was already advanced, and I was no longer accustomed to the fact that to go up high is to go back a season. The snow up there consoled me for the squalor in the valley.

Then I realized that I had just repeated one of my father's typical gestures. How many times had I seen him while driving lean forwards and look up at the sky? To check the state of the weather, or to study the side of a mountain, or to just admire its outline as we passed it. He placed his hands together high up on the steering wheel and rested his temple on them. I repeated the gesture, aware this time of the similarity, imagining myself as my father at forty, having just turned into the valley, with my wife sitting beside me and my son on the backseat, looking for a good place for the three of us. I imagined my son sleeping. My wife was pointing out villages and particular houses, and I was pretending to be listening. But then as soon as she was looking the other way I would lean forward and look up, heeding the powerful call of the peaks. The more towering and menacing they looked, the more I liked them. The snow up there was most promising. Yes, perhaps on that particular mountain there would be a good place for us.

The little road that climbed up to Grana had been asphalted, but as for the rest my mother was right, it seemed as if nothing had changed at all. The ruined buildings were still there, and so too were the stables, the haylofts, the piles of manure. I left the car in the usual place and went into the village on foot in the dark, letting myself be guided by the sound of the drinking fountain, finding my way to the stairs and the door of the house, its big iron key still in the lock. Once inside I was greeted by the old smell of smoke and damp. In the kitchen I opened the stove door and found a small pile of still faintly glowing embers: I put in some of the wood that had been stacked nearby and blew until the fire was kindled again.

Even my father's concoctions were still in their usual place. He would usually bring a large bottle of white grappa and then flavor it in smaller bottles with the berries, pinecones, and herbs that he collected in the mountains. I chose a jar at random and poured some into a glass to warm myself up. It was very bitter, flavored with gentian maybe, and I sat with it next to the stove and rolled a cigarette. Smoking and looking around me in the old kitchen, I waited for the memories to come.

My mother had done a good job there over the course of twenty years: everywhere I looked I could detect her touch, that of a woman with clear ideas about how to make a house homely. She had always liked copper pans and wooden spoons, and never liked curtains that stopped you from seeing outside. On the ledge of her favorite window she had placed a bunch of dried flowers in a pitcher, together with the small radio that she listened to all day and a photo in which Bruno and I were sitting back to back on a larch stump, probably at his uncle's farmstead, with our arms folded, looking like real tough guys. I could not remember who had taken it, or when, but we were wearing the same clothes and adopting the same ridiculous pose: anyone who saw it would have taken it for a portrait of two brothers. I also thought that it was a good photo. I finished the cigarette and threw the butt into the stove. I picked up the empty glass and got up to refill it, and it was then that I saw my father's map still thumbtacked to the wall, though it looked quite different now from how I remembered it.

I went closer to look at it in detail. I saw at once that it had changed from being what it was before—a map of the valley's trails—and that it had become something else altogether, something resembling a novel. Or better still perhaps, a biography: after twenty years there was not a summit, an *alpeggio*, a refuge that my father's felt-tip pen had not reached, and this network of itineraries was so dense as to render the map illegible to anyone else. And now there was not just black ink there. Sometimes it had been marked with red lines, at other times with green. Occasionally the black, red, and green were used together, though most frequently it was the black ink alone that had been used to record the longest excursions. There must have been a key to this code, and I lingered there trying to figure out what it was.

After I had thought about it for a while it began to resemble one of those riddles that my father used to ask me when I was a child. I went to fill my glass and returned to scrutinize the map. If it had been a cryptographic problem like those I had studied at university I would have begun by looking for the most recurrent elements, and for the least frequent. Most frequent were the single black lines, the least frequent those lines where the three colors had been used together. It was the three colors that gave me the key, because I remembered well the time that the three of us—myself, my father, and Bruno—had got stuck on the glacier together. The red line and the green line ended at precisely this point, but the black one continued: from this I understood that my father had completed the rest of the climb alone, on another occasion. The black, of course, was him. The red accompanied him up to our four-thousanders, so could only be me. The green, by a simple process of elimination, was Bruno. My mother had told me that they'd gone walking together. I saw that there were many routes of black and green combined, perhaps even more than of black and red, and I felt a pang of jealousy. But I also felt pleased that during all those years my father had not just gone into the mountains alone. The thought occurred to me that, in some complicated way, this map that was pinned to the wall might contain a message for me.

Later I went into my old room, but it was too cold to sleep there. I took the mattress from the bed, carried it to the kitchen, and put the sleeping bag on top of it. I kept the grappa and tobacco within reach. Before turning off the light I stoked up the fire in the stove, and lay there in the dark listening to the sound of it burning for a long while, without falling asleep.

• • •

Bruno came to get me early the next morning. He was a man I no longer knew, but somewhere inside of him was the boy I knew so well.

"Thanks for the fire," I said.

"Don't mention it," he said.

He shook my hand on the porch and uttered one of those conventional phrases that I had become accustomed to in the past two months, and to which I no longer paid attention. Such phrases would have been of no use between friends, but who could say what Bruno and I were to each other now. His clasp as we shook hands seemed more sincere, his right hand dry and coarse, calloused and with something else about it that was strange and that I didn't understand at first. He sensed my unease and raised it to show me: it was a builder's hand, with the ends of its index and middle fingers missing.

"Have you seen?" he said. "I was messing around with my father's rifle. I wanted to shoot a fox, and boom! I blew off parts of my own fingers."

"Did it burst in your hands?"

"Not exactly. Faulty trigger."

"Ouch," I said. "That must have hurt."

Bruno shrugged his shoulders, as if to say that there were worse things in life. He looked at my chin and asked: "Don't you ever shave?"

"I've had this beard for ten years," I replied, stroking it.

"I tried to let mine grow once. But I had a girlfriend, you know how it is."

"She didn't like your beard?"

"That's right. On you it looks good. You look like your father."

He smiled as he said this. Since we were trying to break the ice I tried to pay no attention to the phrase, and returned his smile. Then closed the door and went with him.

The sky in the deep valley was low and overcast with spring clouds. It looked as if it had just stopped raining, and that it could start again at any moment. Even the smoke from the chimneys was struggling to rise: it slipped down the wet roofs and curled up in the guttering. Leaving the village in that cold light I rediscovered every shack, every henhouse, every woodshed, as if no one had touched anything since I'd left. The things that had been damaged I saw soon after, beyond the last house: down below, the bed of the river was at least twice as wide as I remembered it. It looked as if a gigantic plough had recently turned it over. It flowed between wide stony areas that gave it an anemic look, even in this season of thaw.

"Have you seen?" Bruno said.

"What happened?"

"The flood of 2000, don't you remember? So much water came down that we had to be taken out by helicopter."

There was a digger working down there. Where was I in the year 2000? So far away in both body and spirit that I hadn't even been aware of the flooding in Grana. The river was still littered with tree trunks, beams, pieces of cement, wreckage of every kind dragged down from the mountain. On the bends the eroded banks exposed the roots of trees growing in search of soil that was no longer there. I felt very sorry for our poor little river.

A bit higher up, near the mill, I noticed something in the water that raised my spirits: a large white stone in the shape of a wheel.

"So was that also brought down by the water?" I asked.

"Oh no," said Bruno, "I threw that one down before the flood."

"When?"

"I did it to celebrate my eighteenth birthday."

"So how did you manage it?"

"With a car jack."

It made me smile. I imagined Bruno entering the mill with the jack, and the millstone coming out through the door and starting to roll down. I would have loved to have been there.

"Was it good?" I asked.

"It was amazing."

Bruno smiled too. Then we headed off in search of my property.

• • •

We climbed a good deal slower than we used to, since I was not in shape at all and had ended up drinking too much the previous evening. Going up the valley devastated by the flood, where the meadows along the riverbank were reduced to sand and stones, Bruno had to turn around frequently, show his astonishment that I was so far behind, then stop and wait. Between one bout of coughing and another, I said, "Go ahead if you want. I'll catch you up."

"No, no," he said, as if he had set himself a specific task and had a duty to complete it.

Not even his uncle's farmstead looked right: when we passed by it I saw that the roof of one of the huts had caved in, pushing out the wall on which the beams rested. It looked as if a heavy fall of snow would have been enough to finish it off altogether. The bath had been left to rust outside of the stable, and the doors were off their hinges and thrown jumbled against a wall. Just as in the prophecy made by Luigi Guglielmina, the larch saplings were springing up everywhere in the pastures. Who knows how long it had taken them, and what had happened to his uncle. I would have liked to ask Bruno, but he did not stop, so we passed the farmstead and kept going without a word between us.

Beyond the cabins the flood had done the worst damage. Up above, where once the cows used to climb at the height of the season, the rain had brought down an entire piece of the mountain. The landslide had dragged down with it trees and rocks, a mess of unstable material which even after four years gave way beneath our feet. Bruno continued in silence. He led the way with his boots sinking in the mud, jumping from one rock to another, concentrating on keeping his balance while walking across fallen tree trunks, and he did not turn round. I had to run to keep behind him until we were beyond the landslide, the forest welcomed us again, and he finally recovered his speech.

"Few people used to come this way even before," he said. "Now that the path is no longer here, I'm probably the only one who does."

"Do you come here much?"

"Sure, in the evening."

"In the evening?"

"When I fancy a walk after work. I take the head torch with me in case it gets dark."

"Some people go to the bar."

"I've been to the bar. Enough bars already; the woods are better."

Then I asked the forbidden question, the one that could never be uttered while walking with my father: "Is it much further?"

"No, no. It's just that soon we'll find snow."

I had already noticed it in the shadow of the rocks: old snow that had been rained on and would soon turn into slush. But further up, when I lifted my head, I saw that it stained the scree and filled broad expanses of the gorges of Grenon. On the whole of the north side it was still winter. The snow followed the shape of the mountain like a film negative, with the black of the rocks warming in the sun and the white of the snow surviving in the areas of shadow: I was thinking about this when we reached the lake. Just as it had that first time, the lake revealed itself suddenly.

"Do you remember this place?" asked Bruno.

"Of course."

"It's not like in the summer, eh?"

"No."

Our lake in April was still covered by a layer of ice, by an opaque white veined with thin blue cracks, like those that form in porcelain. There was no regular geometrical aspect to this craquelure, or any comprehensible lines of fracture. Here and there slabs of ice had been raised by the force of the water, and along the banks in sunlight you could see the first darker tones, the beginning of summer.

And yet casting our eyes around the basin it seemed as if we were seeing two seasons at once. On this side was the scree, the bursts of juniper and rhododendron, on the other the woods and the snow. Over there the wake of an avalanche came down along the Grenon and ended up in the lake. Bruno headed straight for it: leaving the shore, we began to climb up the snow slope, a frozen crust that almost always held firm beneath our feet, but that sometimes suddenly gave way. When it did so we would sink thigh-deep in snow. Every false step cost us a laborious extraction, and it was only after half an hour of such halting progress that Bruno allowed us to rest: he found a stone wall that emerged from the snow, climbed on top of it, and cleaned off his boots by knocking them together. I sat down without caring about my sodden feet. I had an overwhelming desire to get back in front of the stove, to eat, and to sleep.

"Here we are," he said.

"Where?"

"What do you mean where? At your place."

It was only then that I looked around. Although the snow altered the shape of everything, I could see that where we were standing the slope formed a kind of wooded terrace. A wall of flat, high, and unusually white rock came down onto this plateau, facing the lake. From the snow emerged the remains of three drystone walls, one of which I was sitting on, built from the same white rock. Two short walls and a longer one in front, four meters by seven, just as the land registry map had specified: the fourth wall, which supported the other three, was the rock face itself that had provided the material for their construction. Of the collapsed roof there was no trace. But inside the ruin, in the middle of the snow, a small Swiss pine had begun to grow, having found its way amongst the rubble, and reached up to the height of the walls. So there it was, my inheritance: a rock face, snow, a pile of shaped stones, a pine tree.

"When we first chanced across this place it was September," Bruno said. "Your father said immediately: this is the one. We had seen so many, since I had been going with him on these searches for quite a while, but this one he liked at first sight."

"Was it last year?"

"No, no. It was nearly three years ago. Then I had to find the owners and persuade them to sell. Nobody ever sells anything up here. It's OK to keep a ruin for your entire lifetime, but not to sell it to someone who might actually do something with it."

"And what did he want to do with it?"

"Build a house."

"A house?"

"Sure."

"My father always hated houses."

"Well, it seems like he changed his mind."

Meanwhile it had started to rain: I felt a drop on the back of my hand and saw that it was halfway between rain and snow. Even the sky seemed undecided between winter and spring. The sky hid the mountains and divested things of their mass, but even on such a morning as this I could sense the beauty of this place. A somber, bitter beauty, communicating awesome power rather than tranquillity, as well as a degree of anguish. The beauty of the reverse side.

"Does it have a name, this place?" I asked.

"Yes, I think so. According to my mother it was once called

barma drola. She's never wrong about such things; she remembers all the names."

"So the *barma* is that rock over there?"

"That's right."

"And the *drola*?"

"That means strange."

"Strange because it's so white?"

"I think yes."

"The strange rock," I said, to hear what it sounded like.

I stayed sitting there for a while, to look around me and to reflect on the meaning of this inheritance. My father, the same person who had fled from houses all his life, had cultivated a desire to build one up here. He hadn't been able to do so. But imagining his own death, he had thought of leaving the place to me. Who knows what he wanted from me.

Bruno said: "I'm available for the summer."

"Available for what?"

"To work, no?"

And since I did not seem to understand, he explained: "Your father designed the house, the way he wanted it. And he made me promise that I would build it. He was sitting right where you're sitting now when he asked me."

The revelations kept on coming. The map of the routes, the red and the green that accompanied the black—and I thought that there were many other things that Bruno had yet to tell me. As for the house, if my father had arranged everything in this way I saw no reason not to observe his wishes. Except for one, that is.

"But I don't have any money," I said. My inheritance had already been used up settling my disastrous finances. There was a little left, but hardly enough to build a house with, and I didn't feel like using it for this. I had a long list of deferred wishes to fulfill.

Bruno nodded. He had expected this objection. He said: "All

that we need to do is buy the materials. And even on them I think it's possible to save quite a bit."

"Fine, but who is going to pay you for doing the work?"

"Don't worry about me. This isn't the kind of job you expect to get paid for."

He did not explain to me what he meant, and just as I was about to ask him he added: "It would be useful to have someone to lend a hand. With a laborer I'd be able to finish it in three or four months. What do you say, are you up for it?"

Down in the plains I would have laughed at the suggestion. I would have answered that I didn't know how to do anything, and that I would have been of no help whatsoever. But I was sitting on a wall in the middle of the snow, facing a frozen lake at an altitude of two thousand meters. I had begun to feel a sense of inevitability: for reasons unknown to me my father had wanted to bring me here, to this clearing pummeled by landslides, beneath that strange rock, to work together with this man on these ruins. OK, dad, I said to myself, set me another riddle; let's see what you've prepared for me. Let's see what else there is to learn.

"Three or four months?" I asked.

"Oh sure."

"When do you want to start then?"

"As soon as the snow melts," Bruno replied. Then he jumped down from the wall and began to explain to me how he thought it should be done.

SIX

THE SNOW DISAPPEARED quickly that year. I returned to Grana at the beginning of June, at the height of the thawing season, with the water swelling the river and coursing down from everywhere in the valley, forming short-lived waterfalls and streams which I had never seen before. It seemed as if you could feel it beneath your feet, that snowmelt from the mountains, and even a thousand meters lower down it rendered the earth as soft as moss. As for the rain that fell daily, we decided to ignore it: one Monday morning at dawn we took from Bruno's house a spade, a pickaxe, a large hatchet, a chainsaw, and half a tank of petrol, and with all this gear on our backs we climbed up to my property—to Barma, as we had begun to call it. Although he was carrying the heavier load, I was the one who had to stop every quarter of an hour to get my breath back. I would put down the rucksack and sit on the ground—all the errors that my father had once taught me to avoid—and we would stay there in silence, avoiding each other's gaze while my heart slowed down.

Up above, the snow had given way to mud and dead grass, allowing me to better assess the state that the ruins were in. The walls seemed solid enough up to about a meter of their height, thanks to cornerstones that even the two of us together could not have shifted; but for a meter above that the long wall was leaning outwards, pushed by the beams of the roof before it collapsed; and the short walls were completely unstable, with the last course of stones hanging on precariously at the height of a man. Bruno said that we would have to demolish them almost down to the base. It would be useless to try to straighten skewed walls: much better to simply throw them down and start from scratch.

But first we had to prepare the building site. It was ten in the morning when we entered the ruin and began to free it of all the collapsed rubble inside.

This was mostly made up of shingles that had once been the tiles of the roof, but also of the old flooring that divided the ground floor from the first, and in the midst of all this sodden wood there were beams of six or seven meters in length still jammed into the walls or stuck in the ground. Some had withstood exposure, and Bruno checked to see if they could be reused. We labored a good deal extracting the sound ones and dragging them outside, rolling them beyond the walls on two inclined planks, while the spoiled ones were split and stored away as firewood.

Because of his truncated fingers, Bruno had learned how to use a chainsaw left-handed. He held the wood down with his foot and worked with the tip of the blade, cutting very close to his boot sole and raising a cloud of sawdust behind him. The pleasant smell of burnt wood perfumed the air. Then the piece he was cutting off would fall, and I would collect it for stacking.

I soon got tired. I was still less used to working with my arms than with my legs. At midday we came out of the ruins covered in dust and sawdust. There were four fine larch trunks beneath the big rock wall, cut down a year ago and left there to season: when the time came they would become the beams of the new roof, but for now I used one to sit on.

"I'm worn out already," I said. "And we haven't even started yet."

"We've started all right," Bruno said.

"We'll need a week just to clear up. And to demolish the walls, and to clear the ground around here."

"We might do. Who knows?"

In the meantime we had made a fireplace with stones and lit a small fire with the woodchips for kindling. As hot and sweaty as I was, it was still pleasurable to dry myself in front of a fire. I rummaged in my pockets, found the tobacco, and rolled a cigarette. I offered the packet to him, and he said: "I don't know how. If you do it for me I'll try one."

When I lit it he tried hard not to cough. I could see that he wasn't a smoker.

"Have you been a smoker for long?" he asked.

"I started one summer when I was here. So how old must I have been, sixteen or seventeen."

"Really? I never saw you smoke."

"Because I smoked in secret. I would go into the woods so as not to be seen. Or up onto the roof of the house."

"And who were you hiding from? From your mother?"

"I don't know. I would just hide, that's all."

Bruno sharpened the ends of two small sticks with his penknife. He took some sausage from his rucksack, cut it into pieces, and put them to grill. He also had bread, a black loaf from which he cut two large chunks and gave one to me.

He said: "Look, it doesn't matter how long it takes. If you try to think too far ahead with this kind of work it'll drive you nuts."

"So what should I think about?"

"About today. Look what a beautiful day it is."

I looked around. You needed a degree of optimism to describe it in such terms. It was one of those days in late spring when the wind is always gusting in the mountains. Banks of clouds came and went, blocking the sun, and the air was still cold, as if an obstinate winter was refusing to make its departure. Down below, the lake looked like black silk rippled by the wind. But actually no, it was the other way round: the wind was like an icy hand smoothing out the movements on its surface. I felt like stretching my own out towards the fire, to steal from it a little of its heat.

In the afternoon we continued to extract the rubble until we reached the floor of the ruin: planking which clearly showed the nature of the building. On one side, against the long wall, we found the feeding troughs, while a small gutter in the dead center of the room served as a drain for the manure. The floor was made of planks the width of three fingers, polished by years of contact with the muzzles and hooves of beasts. Bruno said that we could clean them up and use them to build something else, and began to lever them out with the pickaxe. I noticed something on the floor and picked it up. It was a wooden cone, smooth and hollow, similar to the horn of an animal.

"That's used with a scythe stone," Bruno said, when I showed it to him.

"A scythe stone?"

"A stone for sharpening the blade. There's probably another word for it, but who knows what it is anymore. I should ask my mother. I think it's a river stone."

"From the river?"

I felt like a child to whom everything has to be explained. He showed infinite patience with these questions of mine. He took the horn from my hand and held it to his side, then explained: the scythe stone is a smooth, round stone, almost black. It has to be wet to work properly. You hang this from your belt with a little water inside, so that every so often while you are scything you can moisten the stone and sharpen the blade, like this.

He made a sweeping, soft gesture with his arm, describing a half-moon above his head. I could see perfectly the imaginary scythe and the imaginary stone that was sharpening it. Only then did I realize that we were repeating one of our favorite games: I don't know why it hadn't occurred to me before, since we had been in so many ruins just like this one. We would get in through holes in walls that were in danger of collapse. We walked on planks that moved beneath our feet. We would steal a few wrecked items and pretend that they were treasures. We had done it for years.

So I began to see the project on which we were embarked in a slightly different light. Until then I had believed that I was only there for my father's sake: to fulfill his wishes, to assuage my guilt. But at that moment, watching Bruno sharpening the imaginary scythe, the inheritance I'd received seemed more like a compensation or a second chance for our interrupted friendship. Was that what my father had wanted to give me? Bruno took one last look at the horn and tossed it onto the pile of wood set aside for burning. I went over to retrieve it and put it away, thinking that I would find some future use for it.

I did the same with the Swiss pine that had managed to grow in the middle of the ruin. At five, when I was too tired to do anything else, I used the pickaxe to dig around the little tree and extricate it with its roots still intact. Its trunk was thin and twisted due to its efforts to reach the light from out amongst the rubble. With its roots exposed it looked moribund, and I hurried to replant it nearby. I dug a hole at the edge of the clearing, planting it where there was the best view of the lake, treading down firmly the earth that I used to cover its roots. But when I left it there, in the wind to which it was not accustomed, it was blown from side to side. Exposed to the elements from which it had been long protected, it looked like an altogether too fragile creation.

"Do you think it will make it?" I asked.

"Who knows," said Bruno. "It's a strange plant, that one. Strong where it decides to grow, and weak if you put it somewhere else."

"Have you tried before?"

"A few times."

"How did it work out?"

"Badly."

He looked at the ground, the way he did when thinking again about some old story. "My uncle wanted a Swiss pine in front of the house. I don't know why, maybe he thought it would bring him good luck. And he sure needed it, no doubt about that. So every year he would send me to the mountain to get a sapling. But it always ended up getting trampled by the cows, and after a while we stopped trying."

"What do you call it here?"

"The Swiss pine? *Arula*."

"That's it. And it brings good luck?"

"So they say. Perhaps it does if you believe it."

Whether lucky or not, I felt attached to that young tree. I sunk a stout stick next to its trunk and attached it at several points with twine. Then I went to the lake to fill a drinking bottle to water it with. When I got back I saw that Bruno had constructed a kind of low platform beneath the big wall. He had put on the ground two of the old roof beams and nailed on a few salvaged planks. Then he took from the rucksack a small rope and a rainproof sheet of the kind used in Grana to protect the hay in the fields. With two wooden stakes he attached two corners of the sheet to a crack in the rock and attached the other two to the ground, thus making a kind of shelter beneath which he put the rucksack and provisions.

"Are we leaving this stuff there?" I asked.

"We're not leaving it, I'm staying there too."

"What do you mean you're staying?"

"I mean that I'm sleeping here."

"Sleeping there?"

This time he lost patience, and replied brusquely: "I can't just lose four working hours a day, can I? A builder stays on site Monday to Saturday. The laborer goes back and forth with the materials. That's how it's done."

I looked at the bivouac that he'd constructed. Now I understood why his rucksack had been so full.

"And you want to sleep in there for four months?"

"Three months, four months, whatever it takes. It's summer. On Saturday I can go down and sleep in a bed."

"So shouldn't I stay here too?"

"Maybe later. There are still a lot of materials to bring up. I've borrowed a mule."

Bruno had thought long and hard about the work that was before us. I was improvising; he certainly wasn't. He had planned every phase, both my tasks and his, all the various stages and a timetable for them. He explained where the material had been prepared, and what I would have to bring up to him the next day. His mother would show me how to load the mule.

He said: "I'll expect you at nine in the morning. At six you'll be free to go. If it's all right by you, that is."

"Of course it's all right by me."

"Do you think you can do it?"

"Sure."

"Good on you. So I'll be seeing you then."

I looked at the time: it was six-thirty. Bruno took a towel and a bar of soap and headed uphill, to wash at some place that he knew. I looked over the ruin, which seemed just the same as we'd found it that morning, except that now it was empty inside, and outside of it there was a fine stack of wood. I thought that it wasn't bad for a first day's work. Then I took my rucksack, said goodbye to my tree, and began walking towards Grana.

• • •

There was an hour that I loved more than any other in this month of June, and it was precisely the one during which I descended alone at the end of the day. In the morning it was different: I was in a rush, the mule would not take my orders, my only thought was to get up there. In the evening, instead, there was no reason to hurry. I left at six or seven with the sun still high in the bottom of the valley and with no one expecting me at home. I walked calmly, with my thoughts slowed by tiredness and the mule following behind without needing any prompting from me. From the lake down to the landslide, the rhododendrons were in bloom on the flanks of the mountain. At the Guglielmina farmstead, around the deserted buildings I startled roe deer foraging in the abandoned pastures; bolt upright with their ears at attention, they would look at me in alarm for an instant, then flee to the woods like thieves. Sometimes I stopped there for a smoke. While the mule grazed, I would sit on the larch tree stump where the photo of Bruno and me had been taken. I would contemplate the farmstead and the strange contrast between the entropy of human things and the resurgence of spring: the three buildings were falling into decline—their walls curving like elderly backs, their roofs succumbing to the weight of winters—while everywhere around them was awash with burgeoning herbs and flowers.

I would like to have known what Bruno was doing at that time. Had he lit the fire, or was he walking alone towards the mountain, or did he keep working until dark? In many ways the man that he had become surprised me. I had expected to find if not the double of his father then that of one of his cousins, or of the bricklayers I used to see him with at the bar. Instead he had nothing at all in common with these people. He seemed to me like someone who at a certain point in life had given up on the company of others, that he had found a corner of the world and retreated into it. He reminded me of his mother: I often came across her, in those days, when I was loading up of a morning. She showed me how to fasten the packsaddle, how to secure the planks or the tools on the flanks of the mule, how to goad him on when he refused to budge. But she had not uttered a word about my return, or about the work that I was doing with her son. Ever since I was a child it seemed that nothing in our lives was of interest to her, that she was happy in her own place, and that other people passed by her like the seasons. I wondered, though, whether she did not conceal feelings of an altogether different kind.

I would take the path along the river, and reaching Grana, would tie the mule up next to the house, light a fire, and put a saucepan of water on to boil. If I'd remembered to buy one I would open a bottle of wine. In the larder I had only pasta, conserves, and a few tins for emergencies. After the first two glasses I felt completely exhausted. Sometimes I would throw in the pasta and fall asleep while it was cooking, and find it later that night—the stove gone out, the bottle half-drunk, my supper reduced to an inedible mess. So I would open a tin of beans and devour them with a spoon, without even bothering to tip them from the tin. Then I would stretch out on my mattress beneath the table, zip myself into the sleeping bag, and instantly fall back into a deep sleep.

• • •

Towards the end of June my mother arrived with a friend. Her friends were taking turns keeping her company throughout the summer, though she did not seem to me to have the air of an inconsolable widow. Yet she told me herself that she was happy to have someone close to her, and I noticed the silent intimacy that she shared with this other woman: they spoke together infrequently in my presence, understanding each other with a glance. I saw them sharing the old house with a mutual ease that was more precious than words. After the meager funeral of my father I thought a lot about his loneliness, that kind of perpetual conflict between himself and the rest of the world: he had died in his car without leaving a single friend to mourn his absence. But with my mother I could see the fruits of a long life spent cultivating relationships, caring for them like the flowers on her balcony. I wondered if you learn and develop such a talent, or whether you just have it, or not, at birth. Whether there was still time for me to learn.

So now when I came down the mountain I found not just one but two women to care for me, the table laid, clean sheets on the bed: no more sleeping bag and beans. After supper my mother and I would linger in the kitchen to talk.

Such talk came easily to me with her, and on one occasion I told her that it was like going back to old times there together—only to discover that her own memories of those evenings we shared were quite different from mine.

In her mind, I had hardly ever spoken. She remembered me as absorbed in a world of my own that it was impossible to penetrate, and from which she rarely received any communication. She was only too happy, now, to have the opportunity to make up some ground between us.

At Barma Bruno and I had begun to build the walls. I described to my mother the way in which we were working, since she seemed keen to hear about what I was learning as a laborer. Each wall was actually made of two parallel rows of stones, separated by a space which we filled with smaller ones. Every so often a large stone was put in place across the gap, joining the two rows together. We used cement as little as possible, not for ecological reasons but because I had to carry it up there in sacks, each weighing twenty-five kilos. We would mix the cement with sand from the lake and would pour the mixture between the stones, so that from the outside it could hardly be noticed. For many days I had been going back and forth between Barma and the lake with the sand: there was a small beach on its far shore, where I would fill the mule's saddlebags. I really liked the idea that it was this sand that was holding the house together.

My mother listened carefully, but she was not really interested in the carpentry.

"So how are you getting on with Bruno?" she asked.

"It's strange. Sometimes I feel like I've known him forever, but then I think that I know next to nothing about him."

"What's so strange about it?"

"The way that he speaks to me. He's very kind to me. More than kind, actually, he's affectionate. I didn't remember that side of him. It always strikes me as something I don't really understand."

I threw a piece of wood into the stove. I felt like having a cigarette. But I was embarrassed to smoke in front of my mother, and even though I would have liked to rid myself of that stupid secret, I couldn't bring myself to do so. I went to pour myself a little grappa instead. Grappa was different; there was no embarrassment involved.

When I sat back down my mother said, "Well, you know, Bruno was very close to us during these years. At certain times he was here every evening. Dad helped him a lot."

"Helped him in what way?"

"Not in a practical sense. How can I put it? Yes, on occasion he did lend him money, but that wasn't it. At a certain point Bruno fell out with his own father. He never wanted to work with him again; I think he didn't even see him for years. So if he needed any advice he would come here. He had real faith in what your father had to say."

"I didn't know that."

"And he always asked after you; how you were, what you were up to. I told him what you had written in your letters. I never stopped giving him news about you."

"I didn't know that," I repeated.

I was finding out what happens to the person who leaves: life goes on for the others without him. I imagined their evenings together when Bruno was twenty years old, twenty-five years old, and was there in my place, talking with my father. Maybe it would not have happened if I had stayed, or perhaps we would have shared those moments; more than jealousy I felt regret for not having been there. I felt as if I had missed out on important things, busying myself with others so inconsequential that I could hardly remember what they were.

• • •

We finished the walls and went on to construct the roof. It was already July when I went to the blacksmith in the village to collect the eight steel brackets that Bruno had ordered, made to his own design, together with a few dozen foot-long expansion screws. I loaded these materials onto the mule, together with a small generator, some more petrol, and my old climbing gear. Once everything had been delivered I went to the top of the rock wall, where I had never been before then. There were four larch trees up there. I secured myself to one of the biggest and lowered myself halfway down using a double rope, armed with an electric drill—then spent the rest of the day between the instructions shouted by Bruno from below, the humming of the generator, and the deafening shriek of the drill as it penetrated the rock. Four screws were necessary for each bracket, which meant thirty-two holes in all. According to Bruno these numbers were crucial: the whole viability of the roof depended on them. In the winter the rock would constantly shed snow, and he had thought long and hard about the specifications, in order to construct a roof that could withstand these blows. Several times I pulled myself up the rope, shifted the anchor point a bit further on, and slid back down to where he was indicating to drill the rock. Towards evening the eight brackets had all been fixed in place, aligned at regular intervals of four meters in height.

Our days would end with the beer that I now squeezed into the rucksack in the morning along with our provisions. We sat down in front of the fireplace that was blackened by ash and embers. I, in contrast to it, was white: covered in dust, hands aching from using the rock drill. I was proud that Bruno had decided to entrust me with that work.

"The problem with snow is that you never know how heavy it might get," he said. "There are calculations with which you can work out the load borne, but it's best to double everything."

"What calculations?"

"Well, a cubic meter of water weighs ten quintals, right? Snow can weigh between three and seven, depending on how much air it contains. So if a roof was to withstand snow to a depth of two meters, you would have to allow for a weight of fourteen quintals. I double it."

"So how did they used to work that out in the past?"

"In the past they used to shore everything up. In the autumn, before leaving. They would fill the house with poles reinforcing the roof. Remember those short, thick trunks that we found? But it looks as if one winter even the poles failed to do the job, or who knows, perhaps they forgot to put them in place properly."

I looked at the tops of the walls. I tried to imagine the snow that had accumulated up there suddenly becoming detached and falling. It was some fall.

"Your father really enjoyed discussing this kind of problem."

"Oh, really?"

"How wide a plank needs to be, at what distance from each other they need to be spaced, what is the best wood to use. Pine isn't right because it's too soft. Larch is stronger. It wasn't enough for him to be told what was to be used; he always wanted to know the reasons behind everything. The fact is that one grows in the shade, the other in the sun: it's the sun that hardens the wood; shade and water make it soft and unsuitable for beams."

"Yes, I can believe that he liked to know such things."

"He had even bought himself a book. I would tell him: don't bother, Gianni, we can go and ask some old builder. I took him to see my old boss once. We took our plans to him, and your father brought along a notebook in which he wrote everything down. Though I suspect that afterwards he went to double-check everything with his book, since he didn't trust people much, did he?"

"I don't know," I said. "I think he did."

I hadn't heard my father's name since the day of the funeral. I was glad to hear it uttered by Bruno, even though it seemed to me at times that we had known two altogether different people.

"Are we raising the beams tomorrow?" I asked.

"First we've got to cut them to size. And shape them to fit the brackets. To lift them we'll need the mule; let's see how it goes."

"Do you think it will take a long time?"

"I don't know. One thing at a time, no? First the beer."

"OK. First the beer."

• • •

In the meantime I had been getting back in shape. After a month of taking the road down every morning I was beginning to rediscover my former speed. It seemed to me that the grass in the fields along the way was getting thicker each day, the river water calmer, the green of the larches more vivid: and that for the woods the arrival of summer was like the end of a turbulent adolescence. It was also the period in which I used to arrive, as a boy. The mountain took on again the aspect with which I was most familiar, from the time when I thought that the seasons hardly changed up there and that there was a permanent summer awaiting my return. In Grana I would find the workers preparing the stables, moving things around with tractors. In a few days' time they would take the herds up, and the lower reaches of the valley would be repopulated again.

Now nobody would be going higher anymore. There were another two ruins near the lake, not far from the road that I used going to and fro. The first, besieged by nettles, was in the same state as I had found my own property in the spring. But the roof had only partially collapsed, and taking a look inside, I found the same sad spectacle: its one small room had been vandalized, as if the owner had wanted on leaving it to take revenge for the miserable life lived there, or as if successive visitors had searched fruitlessly for anything of value. There remained a table, a wonky stool, crockery thrown amongst the rubbish, and a stove that still looked good to me, and that I intended to go back and salvage before everything was buried under another collapse. The second ruin, on the other hand, was barely the memory of a much older and more sophisticated building: the first could not have been more than a hundred years old; this one must have been built at least three centuries ago. It wasn't a simple, small stable building but a large Alpine farmstead made up of separate structures, almost like an entire small village, with external stone staircases and roof beams of mysteriously imposing dimensions—mysterious because the trees big enough to make them grew hundreds of meters lower down, and I couldn't imagine how they had been carried there. There was nothing left inside the houses except the walls that remained standing, scoured by the rain. Compared to the shacks I was familiar with, these ruins seemed to speak of a more aristocratic civilization that had exhausted itself in a period of decadence before becoming extinguished altogether.

Going up, I liked to stop for a moment on the shore of the lake. I would bend down to touch the water and test the temperature with my hand. The sun which illuminated the summits of the Grenon had not yet reached the basin, and the lake still had a nocturnal aspect, like a sky no longer dark but not yet light. I could no longer remember clearly why I had distanced myself from the mountain, or what else I had found to love when I had ceased to love it there—but it seemed to me, going back up alone every morning, that I had gradually begun to make my peace with it.

In those July days Barma resembled a sawmill. I had delivered various loads of planks, and now the terrace was crowded with stacked wood: two-meter-long planks of pine still white and perfumed with resin. The eight beams were suspended between the rock face and the long wall, fixed to the iron brackets, inclined at thirty degrees and supported in the middle by a long beam of larch. Now that the skeleton of the roof was in place I could imagine the finished house:

its door faced west and it had two fine north-facing windows that looked towards the lake. Bruno had wanted them to be arched, losing entire days shaping with mallet and chisel the stones that surrounded them. Inside there would be two rooms, one per window. From the two floors of the old building, with the stable below and living room above, we wanted to make only one that would be taller and more spacious. Though it proved to be beyond me as yet, I would sometimes try to visualize the light that would come into it.

On arriving, I would rekindle the embers in the fireplace by throwing in a few dry twigs, fill a small pan with water, and put it on the fire. From the rucksack I would take out fresh bread and a single tomato—one of those that Bruno's mother had managed to grow miraculously at an altitude of thirteen hundred meters. In search of the coffee I would poke my head inside the bivouac and find the sleeping bag disheveled, a candle stump melted onto a plank, a half-open book. Glancing at the cover I smiled at seeing the name of its author: Conrad. From all the schooling that my mother had given him, Bruno had retained a passion for novels about the sea.

He would come out of the house as soon as the smell of the fire reached him. He was in there measuring and cutting the rafters for the roof. He looked wilder as the week progressed, and if I had lost my sense of time I could tell what day of the week it was by the length of his stubble. At nine he was already deep into his work, absorbed by thoughts from which he would only emerge with difficulty.

"Oh," he would say, "you're here."

He would raise his hand and give me his truncated salute, then join me for breakfast. With his knife he would cut a chunk of bread and a slice of *toma*. The tomato he ate as it was—without cutting it and without salt or anything else—staring at the building site and thinking about the work that lay ahead.

SEVEN

IT WAS THE SEASON of return and of reconciliation, two words I thought about frequently as the summer ran its course. One evening my mother told me a story about herself, my father, and the mountain, about the way in which they had met and ended up marrying. It was odd to be hearing about it so late, given that it was the story of how our family originated, and therefore of how I came to be born. But when a boy I was too young for this kind of story, and after that had stopped wanting to hear: at twenty I would have put my hands over my ears rather than listen to family reminiscences, and even on this evening my first reaction was one of reluctance. Yet one side of me looked with affection on these things that were unknown to me. As I listened I gazed out at the opposite flank of the valley, in the penumbra of nine in the evening. It was thick with fir trees on that side, a wood without clearings that descended emphatically all the way to the river. Only a long gorge cut through it with a lighter line, and it was this that held my eye.

As my mother's story unfolded I began to feel something quite different. I know this story already, I thought. And it was true that in my own way I did know it. For years I had collected fragments of it, like someone who possesses pages torn from a book and has read them thousands of times in random order. I had seen photographs, listened to conversations. I had observed my parents and their way of dealing with things. I knew which arguments ended abruptly in silence, which others were drawn out, and which names from the past had the power to sadden or to move them. I had all the elements of the story at my disposal but had never managed to reconstruct the narrative in its entirety.

After I had been looking outside for a while I saw the does that were waiting there on the other side. In the gorge there must have been a vein of water, and every evening just before dark they would leave the wood to drink from it. From this distance I could not see the water, but the deer showed that it was there. They came and went along their own track, and I watched them until it was too dark to see anything anymore.

• • •

This was the story: in the fifties my father was the best friend of my mother's brother, my uncle Piero. They had both been born in 1942, and were five years younger than she was. They had met as children, on the campsite to which the village priest would take them. In the summer they would spend a whole month in the Dolomites. They slept in a tent, played in the woods, learned how to be in the mountains and to fend for themselves, and this was the life that had made them such close friends. I could understand that, no? my mother said. Yes, it was not at all difficult to imagine them.

Piero did extremely well at school; my father had stronger legs and a stronger character. Actually, though, the contrast was not so simple: in some respects my father was the more fragile of the two, and he was also the one who could touch others with his enthusiasm—he was the most imaginative as well as the most restless. His high spirits when in company were infectious, and partly because of this, partly because he was living at boarding school, he soon became a regular at my mother's home. To her he had seemed like a boy with too much energy to burn, like someone who needed to run faster than others in order to use it up. The fact that he was an orphan counted for nothing in those days. It was so common after the war, just as it was common to take in somebody else's son—the son of a relative, perhaps, or of someone who had emigrated, who knows where. In the farmhouse there was no shortage of room, or of work either.

It was not that my father was in need of a practical arrangement. He didn't lack a roof over his head: what he lacked was a family. And so it was that at sixteen or seventeen years old he was always there, Saturdays and Sundays—and every day in the summer for the harvest, the winemaking, the hay cutting, the woodcutting in the forest. He liked to study. But he also liked the outdoor life. My mother told me about when they had challenged each other to press I don't know how many hundreds of kilos of grapes with their feet, of their youthful discovery of wine and of the day they had been found hiding in the cellar, completely drunk. There were so many anecdotes of this kind, she said, but she wanted to make one thing clear: this relationship did not begin and develop by chance. There was a specific mover behind it. The priest, the one from the mountain who was a friend of my grandfather, had for years taken girls and boys camping, and had kept a keen eye on my father to see if he would bond with the others. My grandfather had in turn agreed to welcome this orphan into his own home. It would also be a way of providing for his future.

• • •

Piero was similar to me, my mother said. He was taciturn, reflective. He had a sensitivity that made him able to understand others, and which at the same time made him a bit vulnerable around anyone with a character stronger than his own. When the time came to go to university, he was in no doubt as to his choice of subject: he had always wanted more than anything else to become a doctor. And he would have made a good doctor, my mother said. He had what it took to be one, a talent for compassion and for listening. My father on the other hand was less interested in people than he was in the material world: in earth, fire, air, water; he liked the idea of being able to plunge his hands into its material components and to find out what they were made of. Yes, I thought, that was him all right. That was how I remembered him, fascinated by every grain of sand and crystal of ice, altogether indifferent to people. I could easily imagine the passion with which, at nineteen, he had embarked on his study of chemistry.

In the meantime he and Piero had begun to go into the mountains by themselves. Almost every Saturday, from June to September, they would take the bus for Trento or Belluno, then hitchhike back up the mountain. They spent the nights in meadows, or sometimes in a hayloft. They had no money with which to buy anything. But then neither did anyone else who went into the mountains in those days, my mother said: the Alps were a poor man's North Pole or Pacific Ocean, the destination of young people like them who were in search of adventure. Of the two it was my father who studied the maps and planned new routes. Piero was more cautious, but also more obstinate. He was difficult to convince in the first place, but even more difficult to dissuade halfway, and was the ideal companion for my father, who had a tendency to give up as soon as things did not go according to plan.

Then their paths in life diverged. The chemistry degree was shorter than the one in medicine: my father graduated first, and in '67 went to do his military service. He ended up in the Alpine artillery, dragging cannon and mortar up the mule tracks of the Great War. His degree earned him the rank of NCO, or *Sergeant of Mules*, as he called it: he didn't spend much time in barracks that year, but spent almost the entire time moving from valley to valley with his company. He discovered that he did not dislike this kind of life at all. Whenever he came back he seemed older, both in comparison to the young man who had left and to Piero, who was still spending whole days buried in his books. It was as if he had been the first to taste something harder and more real, and that he liked the taste. He had experienced, albeit in a grappa-induced fog, the long marches and encampments in the snow. And it was about the snow that he would talk to Piero when on leave. About its different forms, its mutable character, its language. In one of those bursts of enthusiasm to which he was prone as a young chemist, he had fallen in love with a new element. He would say that the mountain in winter was another world entirely, and that they should go there together.

• • •

And so it was that during the Christmas of '68, soon after his discharge from the military, he and Piero inaugurated their first winter season. They managed to borrow from someone the skis and sealskins. They began by going again to the places they knew best, except that now, rather than staying out under the stars, they had to pay to sleep at the refuges. My father was super fit, my uncle much less so since he had spent the last year preparing for his final exams. But he was as enthusiastic as my father about making new discoveries. They barely had enough money for food and board, let alone to employ an Alpine guide, so their technique was what it was. And in any case, according to my father, going up was just a question of having good legs—and you could always find a way of getting down. Little by little they were even developing a style of their own. Until, that is, they decided to head in March for a fork of the Sassolungo, and found themselves crossing a slope in the afternoon sun.

I could see vividly the scene that my mother was describing, however many times she must have told it before. My father was up ahead a short distance, and had removed a ski to prepare for the assault, when he felt the ground giving way beneath his feet. He heard a rustling, like the sound that a wave makes retreating over sand. And it really did seem as if the whole slope that they had just traversed was in the process of retreating downwards. Very slowly, at first: my father went down a meter, shifted to the side, and managed to grab hold of a rock, and watched his ski continue sliding on down. Piero, who had been on the steepest and smoothest part of the slope, was going down too. My father saw him lose his balance and slide on his belly, looking up, with his hands scrabbling for purchase that was not there. Then the bank of snow gathered speed and momentum. This was not the dry snow of winter which plummets in powdery clouds—it was the damp spring snow that goes down rolling. Rolling and gathering until it encounters an obstacle, and it buried Piero with hardly an impact: it just went over him and continued its descent. Two hundred meters below the slope flattened out, and it was only there that the avalanche stopped.

Even before it had done so my father ran down in search of his friend, but could not find him. Now the snow was hard: heavy snow compacted by the fall. He wandered on the avalanche calling out, searching everywhere for any sign of movement. But the snow was completely still again, even though it was less than a minute since it had moved. In the months that followed my father would tell it like this: it was as if some great beast had been disturbed in its sleep, merely growled, and then shaken off its irritation before settling down to sleep again in a more comfortable place. As far as the mountain was concerned, nothing had happened.

The only hope, something that happens in a few rare cases, was that Piero had created an air pocket beneath the snow in which he was still able to breathe. In any case my father did not have a shovel, so he took the only sensible course of action open to him: he started towards the refuge where they had slept, only to find himself sinking in softer snow. So he turned round again, retrieved the one remaining ski, and managed somehow to get down with it—despite sliding in short bursts and frequently falling, it was still much better than sinking at every step. He reached the refuge midafternoon and called the emergency services. By the time they got there it was already dark, and they found my uncle the next morning, dead beneath a meter of avalanche, suffocated by the snow.

• • •

It was immediately clear to everyone that it was all my father's fault. Who else could they have blamed? Two facts proved the extent to which they were badly underprepared for winter: they were ill-equipped and had been up there at completely the wrong time. It had recently snowed. It was far too warm to attempt the crossing of a slope. As the more experienced of the two, my father should have known this—should have avoided the crossing and been the first to retreat. My grandfather found something unforgivable in his mistakes, and rather than diminishing with time his rage became more deeply rooted. He did not go so far as to shut my father from the house, but he was no longer pleased to see him, and his whole demeanor altered whenever he turned up. Then he started to avoid him. Even a year afterwards, at the memorial Mass for his son, he made sure to sit on the other side of the church from him. At a certain point my father gave up and ceased to disturb him.

And it is precisely at this point in the story that my mother enters the stage. Though in fact she had always been a part of it, albeit as a spectator. She had known my father for what seemed like a lifetime, even if at first she had merely thought of him as the friend of her brother. Then, gradually, he had become her friend as well. They had sung, drunk, walked, harvested grapes, side by side together so many times that, after the accident, they began to meet up to talk: my father was in a terrible state, and to my mother it did not seem fair. It did not seem fair that he had been given the blame for everything and then left alone to shoulder it. They ended up falling for each other, and about a year later they were married. The entire family refused their invitations to the wedding. So they were married without any relatives present, already prepared to leave for Milan where their lives would begin again. With a new house, new jobs, new friends, new mountains. I was also part of this new life: in fact, my mother said, this was what made sense of all the rest. I with my old-fashioned name: a family name.

• • •

That was all. When my mother had finished her account, I thought about the glaciers. The way in which my father would speak about them to me.

He was not one for retracing his own steps and did not like thinking again about unhappy times, but on certain occasions in the mountains—even on those virginal mountains where no friend had died—he would look at the glacier and something would resurface and come back to him. He put it like this: that the summer erases memories, just like it melts the snow; but the glacier is the snow of winters long past; it is a memory of winter that does not wish to be forgotten. Only now did I understand what he was talking about. And I knew once and for all that I had two fathers: the first had been the stranger with whom I had lived for twenty years in the city, and then burnt my bridges with for another ten; the second was my father as he was in the mountains, the one I had only glimpsed but still knew better than the first: the man who walked behind me on the paths, the lover of glaciers. This other father had left me a ruin to rebuild. So I decided to forget all about the first, and to complete that work to remember him by.

EIGHT

BY AUGUST WE HAD finished the roof of the house. It was made up of two layers of planks separated by a metal sheet and insulation. On the outside it was covered with shingles of larch, superimposed one over another and traversed by grooves down which the water could run off; inside there were matchboards made of spruce. The larch would protect the house from the rain; the spruce would retain the heat. We had decided not to make a hole in it for a skylight so that even at the height of summer the interior would be shaded. The north-facing windows received no direct light, but looking out of them you could see the mountains in front of you, rising on the other side of the lake, shining almost white. Their outcrops of rock and scree were blinding in this season. The light which entered the windows came from there, as if from a mirror. This is how a house built on the reverse side works.

I went outside to look at the far mountains in sunlight. Then turned towards our own, the Grenon, which covered the sky on the other side. I wanted to climb to its top and see what Barma looked like from up there. It had been looming above me every day for two months, but I had not thought of doing this until now: I think that my legs themselves were fostering the desire in me, together with the heat of summer. They were restless again, having regained their strength, and the summer was drawing me towards the heights.

Bruno came down from the roof where he was working on a painstaking job. A layer of lead needed to be fixed between the rock face and the roof, so that the water draining down on rainy days would not find its way into the house. The lining needed to be molded one piece at a time with a hammer, so that it would follow and adhere to every hollow and protrusion. The lead was soft, and with careful work it looked in the end almost as if it had been soldered to the rock, or as if it were one of its own dark veins. In this way the roof and the rock became a single surface.

I asked Bruno about the path leading to the Grenon, and he pointed to a track that went up from the lake along the slope. It disappeared in a thicket of alder, crossed a swampy area, and reappeared further on between flounces of new grass. Behind there, he said, what looked like a ridge actually hid another basin, and another lake smaller than our own. From the lake onwards it was all scree. There wasn't really a path to follow when climbing it, perhaps just a few piled stones indicating the way, or some track used by chamois. But in any case, he said, pointing to a notch in the crest of the summit where a residual snowfield stood out, by keeping my eye fixed on that snow I couldn't go wrong.

"I'd like to take a trip up there," I said. "On Saturday or Sunday maybe if it's sunny."

"Why not go now," he said. "I can do this on my own."

"Are you sure?"

"Of course. Take a day off. Go on, go."

• • •

The lake higher up was different from ours. The last few Swiss pines and larch trees, the last clumps of willow and alder gradually disappeared from the slope, and beyond the ridge the rarefied air of the mountain already blew. The lake was only a greenish pool surrounded by meager grazing and expanses of blueberries. Twenty or so unattended goats were huddled near a ruin and ignored my presence, or almost. The path ended there, amongst the false trails made by the passage of cattle, where the threadbare grass gave way to slabs of scree. I could see clearly the snowfield up above, and I remembered my father's rules: I imagined a straight line between myself and the snow and took it. I could hear his voice in my ears, saying: straight, go up this way.

It had been a long time since I had walked above the treeline. I had never done so alone—but must have learned well, as I still felt at ease moving across the scree. I would see a pile of stones up ahead and make directly for it, moving from stone to stone, instinctively choosing the largest and most stable and avoiding the unstable ones. I felt a kind of give from the rocks, which did not absorb your step like earth or grass but returned some of the force to your legs, enhancing your momentum. So as soon as I had placed a foot on a stone and pushed my weight forwards and upwards the other foot began to move forwards too, and I soon found myself running and leaping across the scree, almost ceding control to my legs and letting them do the work for me. I felt that I could trust them, and that I could not go wrong. I remembered the joy that my father showed as soon as we had left behind the Alpine meadows and entered into the world of rock. The same joy that I felt now, coursing through my own body.

When I reached the small snowfield I was breathing heavily from the run. I stopped to touch that August snow. It was icy and granular, so hard that you needed to scrape it with your nails, and I gathered together a handful to wipe over my forehead and neck to cool myself down. I sucked on it until I felt my lips sting, then climbed across the last section of scree up to the crest. Now the view opened up for me on the other side of the Grenon, the side that was in the sun, where beneath my feet after a section of rock a long meadow sloped gently down to a group of huts, and to grazing dotted by cattle. It seemed as if I had suddenly descended a thousand meters, or had found myself in another season. In front of me the full light of summer and the sound of the lively cattle; behind me, when I looked back, a shadowy, sombre autumn of damp rock and patches of snow. From up here the two lakes were twinned by the perspective. I looked for the house that Bruno and I were building, but perhaps I was too high up—or perhaps it was too well blended-in to be distinguished from the mountain that supplied the material from which it was made.

The piles of stone markers continued beneath the ridge, along a good ledge. But I felt like climbing, and seeing no great difficulties ahead of me decided to reach the summit this way. For the first time in years I placed my hand on the rock, selected footholds, and heaved myself up. Although it was an easy climb, the old maneuvers demanded my complete concentration. I had to think again about exactly where to place each hand and foot, using balance rather than force, trying to stay light. I soon lost all sense of time. I was oblivious to the surrounding mountains, and to the two contrasting worlds that plummeted beneath me: only the rock face directly in front of me existed, only my feet and my hands. Until I reached a point at which it was impossible to climb further, and only then did I realize that I was at the summit.

Now what? I thought. There was a mound of stones on the crest. Beyond this rudimentary monument Monte Rosa had appeared, its glaciers outlined against the sky. Perhaps I should have had a beer with me with which to celebrate, but feeling neither exultation nor relief I decided to stay only as long as it would take to smoke a cigarette, bid farewell to my father's mountain, and then head back down.

I still knew how to recognize each one of the peaks. I observed them while smoking, from east to west, and remembered all of their names. I wondered how high I'd reached, and thinking that I must have passed the three thousand meter mark without any adverse effects on my stomach, I began to look around for any marker giving the altitude. I saw that jammed into a mound of stones there was a metal box. I knew immediately what would be inside. I opened the lid and found a notebook inside a plastic bag, which had not wholly succeeded in protecting it. Its ruled pages had the texture of paper that had dried after getting wet. There were also a couple of pens inside, with which those rare climbers to this point had left a thought, or sometimes just a name and date. The last entry had been made over a week ago. I leafed through its pages and saw that no more than ten people a year had climbed this barren mountain, which cast its shadow over my house and which I already thought of as mine, and that its record of these climbers therefore went back over many years. I read many names, and hardly impressive comments. It seemed to be the case that after so much exertion nobody could find the words with which to express what they felt: those who tried left only some poetic or "spiritual" banality. I leafed backwards through the notebook somewhat irritated by humankind, and did not know what I was looking for until I found it: two lines, from 1997. I recognized the handwriting. And the spirit behind the words. He had written: *Climbed up from Grana in 3 hours and 58 minutes. Still in great shape! Giovanni Guasti*.

I spent a long time staring at my father's words. The ink blurred by water, the signature less legible than the two phrases that preceded it. It was the signature of a man who had been used to signing his name frequently—no longer really a name, just an automatic gesture. Concentrated into the exclamation mark was all the good humor that he had felt that day. He had been alone, or so it seemed from the notebook, and so I imagined him climbing over the scree and coming out on the summit just as I had done. I was sure that he must have been keeping an eye on the time, and that at some point he must have started to hurry. He would have wanted at all costs to get there in under four hours. He felt good up there at the top, proud of the strength of his legs and elated to see his luminous mountain again. I thought of tearing out the page to keep, but then it seemed as sacrilegious as taking away a stone from the summit.

I carefully wrapped the notebook in the plastic, placed it back inside the box, and left it there.

• • •

In the weeks that followed I found other messages from my father. I would study the map of his routes and go in search of him on less noble peaks, those neglected ones lower down the valley. On Monte Rosa towards the August bank holiday processions of roped parties could be made out on the glaciers, and climbers from all over the world crowded into the refuges—but where I went I saw no one, except for the odd solitary climber of my father's age or older. When I overtook them it seemed like I was meeting him. And for them I think that it was like encountering a son, since they would watch me approach and stand aside saying: "Make way for the young!" I could see that these men were pleased if I stopped for a chat, and began to do so. Sometimes I would take the opportunity of sharing a bite to eat. They had all been going back to these same mountains for thirty, forty, fifty years, and preferred just as I did the abandoned high valleys in which nothing ever seemed to change.

A man with white whiskers told me that for him it was a way of revisiting and thinking about his past life. It was as if, starting out on the same old track once a year, he was immersing himself in his recollections and climbing back up again the course of his own memory. He came from the countryside like my father, but his was the rice-growing region between Novara and Vercelli. From the house in which he was born he could see Monte Rosa above the fields, and when he was little had been told that up there was where all the water came from: water for drinking, the water in the rivers, the water with which to flood the rice fields—all the water that was used came from up there, and as long as the ice continued to glisten on the horizon there would be none of the problems caused by lack of water. I liked this old gentleman. He was a widower and missed his wife deeply. He had sunspots on his bald head and a pipe that he filled as we talked. At a certain point he took a canteen from his rucksack, poured two drops of grappa onto a sugar cube, and offered it to me.

"With this you'll go up like a train," he said. And then after a short pause: "Well anyway, there's nothing like the mountains for making you remember."

I too was beginning to realize this.

At the summit I would find a crooked cross, sometimes not even that. I would disturb ibexes that would be startled without ever really fleeing from me. The males would snort their irritation at my presence, the females and little ones sheltering behind them for safety. If I was lucky I would find the metal box hidden at the foot of the cross, or somewhere amongst the stones.

My father's signature was in all the notebooks that I found. He was sometimes laconic, always boastful. I would find myself traveling back ten years just in order to find four words: *Done this one too. Giovanni Guasti.* He must have felt in particularly good shape on one occasion, and been moved by something to write: *Ibexes, eagles, fresh snow. Like being young again.* On another he'd written: *Thick fog all the way to the summit. Old songs. Magnificent view of the interior.* I knew all of those songs, and would like to have been with him, to sing them in the fog. It was part of a melancholy vein that I found in another message from the previous year: *Came back up here after a very long time. It would be wonderful to just stay up here all together, without having to see anyone anymore, without ever having to go back down to the valley.*

"*All* who?" I wondered. And where was I on that day? Who knows whether he had already begun to feel his heart weakening, or what else had happened to prompt him to write such words. *Without ever having to go back down to the valley.* It was the same sentiment that had made him dream of a house at the highest point possible, isolated and impervious, where you could live away from the world. Before putting the notebook back where I had found it, I copied his words and the date into my own notebook. In the books that had been left there I never added anything of my own.

• • •

Perhaps Bruno and I were actually living inside my father's dream. We had found each other again in a pause in our lives: one of those pauses that bring one period to an end and precede another, though we hardly realized this at the time. From Barma we would see the eagles circling below us, the marmots on the lookout before the entrances to their burrows. We would occasionally spot the odd angler or two down at the lake, and the odd walker—but no one looked up in our direction to find us, and we did not descend to greet them. We would wait until everyone had gone before going down of an August afternoon for a swim. The water in the lake was freezing cold, and we would compete to see who could stay under the longest before getting out and racing around the meadows to get the blood circulating in our veins again. We also had a fishing rod, just a pole with a hook, with which I would occasionally manage to catch something using grasshoppers for bait. Then for supper there would be a trout grilled over the fire, and red wine. We would stay in front of the fire, drinking, until it got dark.

By now I was also sleeping up there. I camped out in the unfinished house, directly beneath one of the windows. The first night, I spent long hours gazing from my sleeping bag at the stars and listening to the wind. I would turn over to face inwards, and even in the dark could feel the presence of the rock face, as if it were exerting a magnetic force, or a gravitational one—or like when, with your eyes closed, someone puts a hand close to your forehead and you feel the hand's presence. I felt as if I were sleeping in a cave excavated from the mountain itself.

Like Bruno, I soon became unaccustomed to hurry and to civilization: I reluctantly went down to the village once a week, just in order to buy supplies, and was surprised to find myself back amongst cars after a walk of only a few hours. The shop owners treated me like any other tourist—a slightly more eccentric one, perhaps—and I was content to leave it at that. I felt better when I was back on the path. I loaded the bread, vegetables, salami, cheese, and wine onto the mule, gave him a slap on the rump, and left him to find his own way along the path that he knew now by heart. Perhaps we really could have stayed up there forever without anyone even noticing.

The late August rains came. I remembered them well. These are the days that bring autumn to the mountains: when they are over and the sun comes back, its light is less warm and more oblique, casting long shadows. Those banks of slow-moving, shapeless clouds that now swallowed the peaks had once told me that it was time to leave, and I had protested to the heavens that the summer had only lasted an instant—had it not only just started?—and could not have already flown away like this.

At Barma the rain was flattening the grass in the meadows, breaking the surface of the lake. The drumming and run-off of the rain on our roof blended with the crackling of the fire. At this time we were lining one of the rooms with fir, keeping warm with the stove that I'd salvaged. We had installed it against the wall made from the rock face. The rock behind the stove would gradually warm up and radiate back heat to the rest of the room, and the wood paneling was meant to help in conserving it. But this was to be at some future date: without windows or doors in place the wind blew down our necks, and the rain came in, in diagonal gusts. With work finished for the day, it was pleasant to be inside, watching the stove and feeding the fire with wood that had once been part of the old house.

One evening Bruno talked to me about a project that he had in mind. He wanted to buy his uncle's farmstead. He had been putting aside money for a good while now. His cousins, who were more than happy to rid themselves of the place and their bad memories of it, had come up with a price: Bruno had spent everything he had on a down payment, hoping to borrow the rest from the bank. These months spent in Barma had served as a kind of trial run: now he knew that he could cope. If everything went according to plan he would spend the next summer working in the same way there: he wanted to rebuild the huts, buy some cattle, and in a few years hoped to have the farm up and running.

"It's a nice idea," I said.

"Cows don't cost much now," he said.

"And does it pay to keep them?"

"Not a lot. But that doesn't matter. If it was just about the money I'd stay as a builder."

"You don't like working as one anymore?"

"Sure, I like it. But I always knew that it was a temporary thing. It's something that I can do, but it's not something I was born to do."

"So what were you born to do?"

"To be a man of the mountains."

Uttering this phrase he became serious. I'd only ever heard him use it a few times before, when speaking of his ancestors: the old inhabitants of the mountain that he knew through the woods, the wild meadows, the derelict houses that he had spent a lifetime exploring. Abandoning them had once seemed inevitable to him too, when the only life he could see for himself was the same as for the men of the valley. You had to look down, to where the money was and the work—and not up, to where there was nothing but weeds and ruins. He told me that in the end, on the farmstead, his uncle had stopped fixing anything. If a chair broke he just burned it in the stove. If he saw an invasive plant in the meadow he couldn't be bothered to bend down and uproot it. His father would start cursing if you so much as mentioned the place to him: he would gladly have turned his rifle on the cattle, and the thought that everything there was going to rack and ruin gave him a twisted kind of pleasure.

But Bruno felt himself to be different from this. So different from his father, his uncle, and his cousins that at a certain point he had understood who it was that he did in fact resemble, and from where he had got his desire to heed the call of the mountains.

"From your mother," I said. But not because it had ever occurred to me before: I only saw it now, at this moment.

"Yes," said Bruno. "We're just like each other, me and her."

He paused so I could reflect properly on what he'd said, and then he added: "Except that she's a woman. If I decide to go and stay in the woods no one says anything about it. If a woman does it, she's taken for a witch. If I keep quiet, what problem is there with that? I'm only a man who chooses not to speak. A woman who doesn't speak must be half-crazy."

It was true: we had all thought this about her. I myself had never exchanged with her more than a couple of words. Even now, when I passed by Grana and she gave me potatoes, tomatoes, and *toma* to take back up. A little more stooped and thinner than I remembered, she was nevertheless still for me the strange figure that I had seen up there in the vegetable garden as a boy.

Bruno said: "If my mother had been a man she would have had the life she wanted. I guess that she wasn't really cut out for marriage. Definitely not for marriage with my father. Her only bit of good luck was getting free from him."

"And how did she do that?"

"By keeping her mouth shut. And by staying up there with the chickens. You can't get so angry with someone like that; sooner or later you leave them in peace."

"Is that what she told you?"

"No. Or perhaps she did, in a way. It doesn't matter whether she told me or not, I worked it out for myself."

I knew that Bruno was right. I had understood something similar about my own parents. I began to think over that phrase—*her only bit of good luck was getting free from him*—and wondered whether it could be applied to my mother too. It was always possible, given what I knew about her. Perhaps not really a stroke of luck, but maybe more like a relief. My father had always been a man who filled the room. He was bossy, and he was hard work. When he was around, no one else mattered but him: his character demanded that all of our lives should revolve around his.

"And you?" Bruno asked me after a while.

"What about me?"

"What are you going to do now?"

"Oh, I'm going away, I think. If I can manage it."

"Where to?"

"To Asia maybe. I don't know yet."

I had hardly ever spoken to him about my longing to travel. I was tired of being penniless, especially so since I needed money in order to leave: in the past few years I had spent all my energy just struggling to make ends meet. I didn't miss any of the things that I didn't have, except for the freedom to travel the world. With my father's small inheritance I had paid off my debts and wanted to devise a project that would take me far away from home. I felt like taking a flight somewhere and staying away for a few months, without any clear idea as to what I would do, just to see if I could find some story to tell. I had never done anything like this before.

"It must be great to leave like that," Bruno said.

"Would you like to come?" I asked. I was joking, but not entirely. I was sorry that the work had come to an end. Never before had I felt so at ease with anyone.

"No, it's not for me," he said. "You're the one who comes and goes. I'm the one who stays put. Same as always, right?"

• • •

When it was finished, in September, the house was like this: it had one room made of wood, and one of stone. The wooden room was larger and warmer with the stove, the table, two stools, and a larder. Some of this furniture came from other ruins, salvaged and cleaned up by me with elbow grease and sandpaper; some had been made by Bruno from the old floor planks. Under the roof, against the rock face, there was a loft that could be reached with a ladder—the warmest and most enclosed corner of the house—while the table was placed right under the window, so that you could look outside when sitting there. The stone room was small and cool, and we intended to use it as a cellar, a workshop, and a storeroom. We left in there most of the equipment that we had used, and all of the leftover wood. There was no bathroom, no running water, no electricity, but we had thick panes in the windows and a sturdy front door with a latch but no lock. Only the stone room was under lock and key. The lock was needed to prevent the equipment from being stolen, but the wooden room remained open as was customary in the mountain refuges, in case anyone passing that way should get into difficulty and need shelter. The grass around the house had been mown like a garden's now; the firewood was stacked under a lean-to and my little pine tree looked out towards the lake, even though it did not seem any healthier or more robust to me than on the day that I replanted it there.

On the last day, I went to Grana to collect my mother. She laced on the leather hiking boots that I'd seen her use since I was a child:

she had never had another pair. I thought that she would get tired climbing up there, but she went up slowly, at her own pace, without stopping once, and from behind I could see how she was walking. She kept the same slow but sure rhythm for two hours. She gave the impression that she would never slip or lose her balance.

It made her very happy to see the house that Bruno and I had built. It was a short September day, with little water remaining in the rivers, the grass drying in the meadows, the air no longer the warm air of August. Bruno had lit the stove, and it felt good to be indoors, drinking tea in front of the window. My mother liked the window, and she stayed there gazing out while Bruno and I organized the material that had to be taken down with us. Then I saw her go onto the terrace and look carefully at everything, so that she would remember it: the lake, the scree, the peaks of Grenon, the look of the house. She stood for a good while looking at the inscription that the day before, with mallet and chisel, I had made in the rock wall. I had gone over it with black paint, and it read:

GIOVANNI GUASTI

1942–2004

IN MEMORY IS THE MOST BEAUTIFUL REFUGE

Then she called us to sing a song. It was the song that is sung when a lover of the mountains dies, the song in which you ask God to allow him to continue to go walking in the afterlife. Both Bruno and I knew it. It all seemed just right to me, all done as was fitting. There was one thing still to be said: I had been thinking about it for a while and decided to say it now so that my mother could hear it, so that there would be a witness to remember it: I said that I wanted this house not to be mine, but to be ours. Mine and Bruno's. Both of ours. I was convinced that this was what my father had wanted, that he had left it between us. But above all I wanted it to be this way myself, because we had built it together. From that moment, I said, he should consider it to be his own home, just as much as I considered it to be mine.

"Are you sure?" he asked.

"I am."

"Then it's fine," he said. "Thanks."

Then he removed the embers from the stove and threw them outside. I closed the front door, took the mule's bridle, and told my mother to lead the way, and the four of us set off towards Grana, at my mother's pace.

THREE

A Friend in Winter

NINE

IT WAS AN OLD Nepalese man who told me, afterwards, about the eight mountains. He was carrying a load of hens up the valley below Everest, heading to one of the refuges where they were destined to become chicken curry for tourists: he had a cage on his back which was divided into a dozen separate cells, and the chickens, still alive, were flustered inside them. I had not yet come across a contraption of this kind. I had seen panniers full of chocolate, biscuits, powdered milk, bottles of beer, of whisky and of Coca-Cola, going along the trails of Nepal to cater for the tastes of Westerners, but never a portable hen-house. When I asked the man if I could photograph it he put it down on a low wall, removed from his forehead the band with which he was carrying it and struck a pose, smiling, next to the chickens.

Then while he was getting his breath back we talked for a while. I'd visited the region he came from, which astonished him. He understood that I was not a casual walker, and discovering that I could even string together a few phrases in Nepalese, asked me why I was so interested in the Himalayas. I had a ready answer to that question: I told him that there was a mountain where I had grown up, and to which I was attached, and that it had fostered in me a desire to see the most beautiful mountains in the world.

"Ah," he said. "I understand. You are doing the tour of the eight mountains."

"The eight mountains?"

The man picked up a small stick and drew a circle with it on the ground. You could tell he was used to drawing it; he executed it so perfectly. Then, inside the circle he drew a diameter, and then another perpendicular one bisecting the first, and then a third and a fourth through the point of bisection, thus creating a wheel with eight spokes. I thought that if I had drawn that figure myself I would have started with a cross—that it was typical of an Asian to begin with a circle.

"Have you ever seen a drawing like this?" he asked.

"Yes," I replied. "In mandalas."

"That's right," he said. "We believe that at the center of the earth there is a tremendously high mountain, Sumeru. Around Sumeru there are eight mountains and eight seas. This is the world for us."

While he was speaking he drew outside of the wheel a small peak for each spoke, and then a little wave between one peak and the next. Eight mountains and eight seas. Finally, at the center of the wheel, he drew a crown which I thought might represent the summit of Sumeru. He assessed his work for a moment and shook his head, as if to say that this was a drawing that he had made a thousand times but that of late he had begun to lose his touch a little. Be that as it may, he pointed the stick to the center and concluded, "We ask: who has learned most, the one who has been to all eight mountains, or the one who has reached the summit of Sumeru?"

The chicken carrier looked at me and smiled. I smiled too, because the story amused me and because I thought that I had understood its meaning. He rubbed out the drawing with his hand, but I knew that I would not forget it. Well, I said to myself, this will be a good one to tell to Bruno.

• • •

The center of my world in those years was the house that I had built with Bruno. I would stay there for long periods between June and October, and sometimes would take friends who would immediately fall in love with the place. In this way I had up there the company that I lacked in the city. During the week I lived alone, reading, writing, cutting wood, and wandering around the old paths. I became accustomed to solitude. And I was at ease with it, though not entirely. But on Saturdays during the summer there was always someone who would seek me out there, and then the house ceased to resemble the hut of a hermit, becoming more like one of the refuges that I used to frequent with my father, with wine on the table, the stove lit, friends who would stay up late talking—and that shared isolation from the world that made us all brothers for a night. The refuge was warmed by the fire of this intimacy, and it seemed to me that between one visit and the next it kept its embers glowing.

Bruno was also attracted to the warmth of Barma. I would see him appear on the path towards evening carrying a piece of *toma* and a bottle of wine, or hear his knock on the door when it was dark already, as if it was quite normal up there, at two thousand meters, to receive a visit from a neighbor at night. If I happened to have company he would happily join us all at the table. I found him to be more talkative than usual, as if he had been silent too long and had accumulated a lot to say. In Grana he remained confined in his world of building work, books, walks in the woods, silent reflection—and I could understand the urgency with which after a day on the building site he would wash and change, ignore his tiredness and the urge to sleep, and take the path to the lake.

With these friends we would often talk about going to live in the mountains together. We were reading Murray Bookchin and dreaming, or pretending to dream, of turning one of the abandoned villages into an ecological community where we could experiment with our ideas about society. Only in the mountains would it be possible to do this. Only up there would we be left in peace. We knew of other, similar experiments that had taken place throughout the Alps: all short-lived and ending up badly, but the fact that they had failed did not stop us from fantasizing; it gave us instead plenty to discuss. How would we manage for food? What would we do about electricity? How would we build the houses? A little money would still be necessary: how would we earn it? Where would we send our children to school? Assuming, that is, that we wanted to send them to school. And how would we resolve the problem of the family, that enemy of every community—worse even than private property and power?

It was this utopian game that we would play of an evening, at weekends. Bruno, who was actually in the process of building his ideal village, amused himself by demolishing ours. He would say: without cement the houses would not stay up, and without fertilizer even the grass in the meadows won't grow; and I'd like to see you try to cut wood without petrol for a chainsaw. What do you plan to eat during the winter, polenta and potatoes like the old folk? And he would say: it's only you townies who use the word *nature*. And it's as abstract to you as the word itself. We say *wood, meadow, river, rock*, things that we can actually point to. Things that can be used. If they can't be used, we don't bother to even give them a name: it would be pointless to do so.

I liked to hear him talk like this. And I also liked the enthusiasm he had for certain ideas that I had picked up on my travels around the world, especially since he was the only one with the skills to put them into practice. One year he carved out the trunk of a larch tree with a chainsaw, ran fifty meters of tubing from one of the streams that feeds into the lake, and built a fountain in front of the house. In this way we had drinking water and water to wash with, but that wasn't the main idea: under the jet from the fountain he installed a turbine that I had ordered from Germany. A plastic one no bigger than a foot in diameter, resembling a toy windmill.

"Hey, Berio," he said, when our mill wheel started to turn. "Do you remember?"

"Of course I remember."

The system charged a battery with which, in the house, we managed to run a radio and a lightbulb for an entire night. It worked night and day, regardless of the weather—unlike solar panels or wind turbines—and it cost nothing and consumed nothing. It was the water that came down from the mountain and flowed towards the lake that in passing by the house gave light and music to our evenings.

• • •

There was a girl who came up with me in the summer of 2007. Her name was Lara. We had only been together for a couple of months. We had reached the stage which for others would mark the start of a relationship, but which for us was already the end: I had begun to withdraw, to avoid her, and to disappear, so that she would leave me before doing so became too painful. This was a tried and tested system with me, and in those last days she forced me to own up to what I was doing. She was upset for a night, then got over it.

These were enjoyable days, just as soon as we had understood that they would be our last together. Lara really liked the house, the lake, the rocks, and the peaks of Grenon, and liked to go on long walks by herself on the paths around Barma. I was surprised to see how she walked. She was strong legged, at ease with the spartan life that we lived up there. In the end I got to know her better during the days we spent there than in the two months that we had been sleeping together. She told me that from her childhood she was used to washing with cold water and drying in front of a fire: she had come from another mountainous region, had left it behind years ago in order to study, and now missed those mountains. Not that she regretted the decision to go to the city. She felt that her relationship with Turin was something of a love story. She had fallen in love with the streets, the people, the nights, the work that she had done there, and the houses in which she had lived: a long, lovely affair that was all but over now.

I told her that I knew exactly what she meant. That something similar had happened to me. She gave me a sad look in which there was both reproof and regret. In the afternoon I watched her go down to the lake where she took off her clothes and swam naked to the rock that resembled a reef, and for a moment I felt that I might have pushed her away from me too soon. But only before remembering what I was like when in a relationship with anyone. After that, I had no second thoughts.

I invited Bruno to supper that evening. He was behind with his project by a whole year, due to delays in securing loans and planning permissions, but had now almost finished renovating the farmstead. He thought of nothing else: he had been struggling with people at the bank and with local council officials; he had two jobs in the winter to earn the money that he spent during the summer and was in that state of complete, almost obsessive, concentration familiar to me from the time I spent with him as his laborer. He spent the whole evening telling us about constructing stables that would meet building regulations, about places for making cheese and cellars for maturing it, about equipment made of copper and steel, and about washable tiles in the old sheds. Things that I already knew about well enough but that Lara did not—and the enthusiasm with which he spoke about them was directed towards her. He amused me, my old friend Bruno, since I had never before seen him trying to impress a woman: he used unusually technical vocabulary, exaggerated his gestures, and kept glancing at her to gauge her reactions.

"He likes you," I told her, after he had left.

"And how do you know that?"

"I've known him for twenty years. He's my best friend."

"I didn't think that you had friends," she said. "I thought that you ran a mile as soon as you caught sight of one."

I did not reply to that. Sarcasm was the lesser of the evils that might come my way. You need style to be left by someone, and she had it.

• • •

I was preparing to leave for a job that autumn when Bruno sought me out in Turin. I was going to the Himalayas for the first time, and I could hardly contain myself. I was surprised to hear his voice at the end of the telephone: partly because neither of us set much store by that means of communication, partly because my mind was already elsewhere.

He got straight to the point: Lara had just gone back to see him. Lara? We hadn't seen each other since those last days in the mountains. Now she had gone up there by herself, wanting to visit the *alpeggio* and to find out more about his work and his plans. Bruno had told her that in the spring his agricultural business would be up and running, that he was thinking of buying thirty cows and using their milk to produce cheese rather than selling it to one of the dairies, and that to do this he would need to employ someone else. It was just what she had been hoping for: she liked the place, had been raised around cattle, and immediately offered herself for the job.

On the one hand Bruno was flattered, on the other worried. He hadn't figured on the presence of a woman up there. When he asked what I thought, I said: "I think that she'll do it well. She's hardheaded."

"I got that," said Bruno.

"And so?"

"What I don't know is how things are between the two of you."

"Oh," I said. "I don't know. We haven't seen each other for two months now."

"Have you fallen out?"

"No. There's nothing between us anymore. I'm happy to see her going up there with you."

"Are you sure about that?"

"Definitely. No problem."

"Then it's fine."

He said goodbye and wished me a good trip. Here, I thought, was a man from another time: who else would have asked permission to do what he was about to do? When I hung up I already knew everything that was about to happen. I was pleased for him. And I was pleased for her. Then I stopped thinking about Bruno or Lara or anyone else, and began to prepare my rucksack for the Himalayas.

• • •

My first journey to Nepal was like a journey back in time for me. A day's drive by car from Kathmandu and fewer than two hundred kilometers from its crowds a narrow, irregular, wooded valley began, with a river below, which you could hear but not see, and villages built up above where the slopes softened in the sunlight. They were connected by mule tracks that rose and fell steeply, and narrow rope bridges suspended over the streams that cut the flanks of the valley like blades. Around the villages the mountain was covered in terraces and rice paddies. Seen in profile, it resembled a staircase with semicircular steps, bordered by low dry stone walls and divided into a thousand smallholdings. October was the harvest season, and climbing up I watched the farmers at work: the women kneeling in the fields, the men beating the husks in the yards to separate the grain from the chaff. The rice was drying on cloths where other, older women sifted it carefully. Children were everywhere. I saw two plowing a field as if it were a game, urging on a couple of emaciated oxen with their shouts and with blows from a stick, and I remembered Bruno's yellow cane from the first time we met.

He too would have liked Nepal. Here they still had wooden plows, river stones to sharpen scythes, and wicker baskets for porters to carry on their backs. Even if I could see that the farmers were wearing trainers, and could hear the sound of radios and televisions, it seemed to me that I had rediscovered, still thriving, the old civilization that had become extinct in our own mountains. Along the route I did not see a single derelict building.

I was climbing up the valley towards Annapurna with four Italian mountaineers. I had been sharing a tent with them for a few weeks now, together with my film camera. I was on a well-paid assignment, and from the outset it had seemed to me like a real stroke of luck. I was intrigued by the prospect of filming a documentary about mountaineering, of seeing what would happen to this group of men under extreme conditions. But what I was discovering as we neared the base camp fascinated me even more. I had already decided to stay on after the expedition, and to make my own trip around the lower levels.

On the second day of walking, at the end of the valley, the summits of the Himalayas appeared. And then I saw how mountains must have been at the world's beginning. Mountains that were newborn, sharply cut, as if just sculpted by creation, not yet eroded by the passage of time. Their snows lit the valley from a height of six or seven thousand meters. Waterfalls plummeted from overhangs and carved the rock faces, detaching from ledges landslides of reddish earth which ended up frothing in the rivers. Up above, oblivious to the tumult below, the glaciers looked out over everything. And it was from up there that the water comes, as the man with the white whiskers had told me. They must have known this well enough in Nepal too, since they had named their mountain after the goddess of harvests and of fertility. Along the path the water was everywhere: the water of the rivers, of the fountains, of the canals, the water of the basins in which the women did their laundry, the water that I would like to have seen in spring, with the rice fields flooded and the valley transformed into a myriad of mirrors.

I don't know if the mountaineers with whom I was climbing noticed these things or not. They were impatient to leave behind the villages and to start planting pickaxes and climbing irons in the ice that was glittering up there. Not me. I walked between porters so that I could ask them about anything that I did not understand: what kind of vegetables were grown in the plots, which kind of wood was burnt in the stoves; to whom the small shrines that we encountered along the way were dedicated. In the woods there were no fir or larch trees, but a strange contorted species that I could not identify, until one of the men told me that they were rhododendrons. Rhododendrons! My mother's favorite plant because it flowered for just a few days, at the beginning of summer, painting the mountain with pink, lilac, and violet, and which here in Nepal produced trees five or six meters high with black bark that flaked off in scales, and had leaves that were as oily as bay leaves. And further up, when the wood came to an end, what appeared was not willow or juniper but a bamboo grove. Bamboo! Bamboo at three thousand meters. There were young men who passed us carrying bundles of swaying bamboo on their backs. In the villages they used them to make roofs, cutting them lengthwise and superimposing the two halves—one concave and one convex—to help with the runoff of rainwater during the monsoon season. The walls were made of stone cemented with mud. About their houses I already knew everything there was to know.

At each of the wayside shrines the porters left a pebble or a bud they had collected in the woods, and advised me to do the same. We were entering sacred territory, and from here on it was forbidden to slaughter or to eat an animal. Now I stopped seeing chickens outside the houses, or goats grazing. There were some other animals, wild ones that browsed on the ledges, with long hair that reached down to the ground: the blue sheep of the Himalayas, someone told me. A mountain with blue sheep; monkeys similar to baboons, glimpsed in the bamboo thickets—and against the sky, moving slowly, the eerie outlines of vultures. And yet I felt at home. Even here, I told myself, where the woods end and there's nothing left but grass and scree, I'm at home. This is the altitude to which I belong, at which I feel best. I was thinking about this when I stepped onto the first snow.

• • •

I went back to Grana the following year with a string of prayer flags, which I hung between two larch trees and we could see through the window of the house. The flags were blue, white, red, green, and yellow—blue for ether, white for air, red for fire, green for water, yellow for the earth—and they stood out against the shade of the wood. I would often watch them of an afternoon, as they tried to come to terms with the wind of the Alps and danced between the branches of the trees. The memories that I had of Nepal were like those flags: vivid, warm, so that my old mountains now seemed more desolate than ever. I would go out walking and see nothing but derelict huts and ruins.

But something new was happening in Grana. Bruno and Lara had been together for a while now: they had not needed to explain how things had developed. He seemed more serious than before, as men can be sometimes when a woman comes into their life. She, on the other hand, had been happily transformed, shaking off the dust of the city together with that air of disappointment I remembered her as having, and of which there was no longer a trace. She had a high-toned laugh, and her skin was flushed from life lived in the open air. Bruno adored her. Here was another version of my friend that I did not know: at the table on the first night, while I was talking about my travels, he could not stop touching her, caressing her, taking every opportunity to place a hand on her leg or shoulder, and even when talking to me he was in constant physical contact with her. In his presence Lara seemed less anxious, less uncertain of herself. She needed only a gesture or a look of reassurance, and it was all: *Are you there? I'm here. But really? Yes, I told you, yes.* Lovers, I thought: it was good that the world contained them, but in the confines of a room they always made you feel superfluous.

During that winter not much snow had fallen, so Bruno decided to go to the *alpeggio*—or to the mountain, as he would say—on the first Saturday of June.

I lent him a hand that day. He had bought twenty-eight dairy cows, creatures that were all already pregnant when they were unloaded from a cattle truck in the piazza in Grana. They were unsettled by the journey, and hurried down the ramp lowing and poking each other with their horns. They would have scattered who knows where if Bruno, his mother, Lara, and I had not been there positioned around the square in order to contain them and calm them down. The truck left. Together with two black dogs of venerable Grana shepherding pedigree we began to climb up the mule track, Bruno in front with his "*Oh, oh, oh! Eh, eh, eh!*" and his mother and Lara further down the line, with me bringing up the rear, doing nothing and enjoying the spectacle. The dogs knew how to do this job to perfection, and would run to reclaim any cows that were slowing things down, barking and nipping them on the flanks until they had rejoined the group. The barking of the dogs, the bellows of protest from the cows, and the noise of their bells drowned out all other sounds, and it seemed to me I was a spectator at a carnival parade or at a kind of resurrection. The herd climbed up the valley past the derelict huts, past the stone walls riddled and undermined by weeds, past the gray stumps of felled larches—like a bloodstream that was beginning to circulate again, bringing a body back to life. I wondered if the foxes and deer that must have been watching us from the woods as we passed could share in the sense of celebration that I felt.

At a certain point in the climb Lara joined me. We had not yet had the chance to speak together, just the two of us, but I think we both thought that we needed to. I don't know why she chose that particular moment, when our words needed to be shouted into the cloud of dust that was enveloping us. She smiled at me and said: "Who would have thought it a year ago?"

"Where were we a year ago?" I wondered. "Oh yes, in a bar in Turin, perhaps." Or in bed together at her place.

"Are you happy?" I asked.

"Very," she said. And smiled again.

"Then I'm happy too," I said, and I knew that we would never raise the subject again.

At that time the dandelions were in flower. They would all open together early in the morning, and then a brilliant yellow was brushed over the mountain, as if it were the sun itself flooding over it. The cows adored these sweet flowers: when we arrived up there they scattered over the pasture as if to a banquet that had been set for them. In the autumn Bruno had uprooted all the bushes that had infested the meadow, so that now it had again the look of a well-kept garden.

"You're not putting up the fence-line?" his mother asked him.

"The fencing's for tomorrow. Today I'm giving them a holiday."

"But they'll ruin the grass," she protested.

"Come on," said Bruno. "They won't ruin anything, don't worry about it."

His mother shook her head. I had heard her use more words that day than I had heard her utter in all the years that I'd known her. She had come up limping, with a stiff leg that she trailed a little, but keeping a good pace. I could not understand how she could be so thin: shrunk within her ample clothing she scrutinized everything, controlled everything, giving both advice and criticism, because there was a right and a wrong way in which everything should be done.

The three buildings seemed to have been restored to a previous era in their existence. A house, a stable, and a storeroom, with walls and roofs of stone, reconstructed perfectly, even though they were now the premises of a modern agricultural enterprise. Bruno went into the cellar and returned with a bottle of white wine, and I recalled the same gesture that his uncle had made all those years ago. He was the master of the place now. We had nothing to sit on. Lara said that they would make a fine table to eat at in the open air, but for now we made our toast standing, at the threshold of the stable, watching the cows as they accustomed themselves to the mountain.

TEN

BRUNO PERSISTED OBSTINATELY in milking the cows by hand. For him this was the only method properly suited to these delicate creatures, prone as they were to becoming nervous and taking fright at the slightest thing. It would take him about five minutes to obtain as many liters of milk from each one: good going, but it meant twelve cows an hour, or two and a half hours of work for the whole herd. This was what got him out of bed in the morning when it was still dark outside. There were no Saturdays or Sundays on the farm, and he could hardly remember the pleasure of sleeping in until late, or of lingering between the sheets with his girl. Yet he loved this ritual and would not see it done by anyone else: he spent the hours between night and day in the warmth of the stable, clearing the sleep from his mind as he worked—and milking the cows was like waking them one by one with a caress, until they were aware of the fragrance of the meadows and the singing of the birds and started to become restless.

Lara would come to him at seven with coffee and a few biscuits. She was the one who would take the herd out to pasture twice each day. He would pour the one hundred and fifty liters of milk together with the same amount from the previous evening, skimmed of the cream that had risen to the surface overnight. He would light the fire under the boiler and add the rennet, and by nine o'clock each morning the mixture would be ready to be strained through cloth and pressed into the wooden molds. Five or six loaves in total: three hundred liters of milk to make no more than thirty kilos of *toma*.

This was the most mysterious phase for Bruno, because he was never sure how it would go. Whether the cheese would form or not, whether it would turn out to be good or bad: this seemed to him an alchemical process over which he had no control. He knew only how to treat the cows well and to carry out every part of the process exactly as he had been taught. With the cream he would make butter, and then wash the boiler, the churns, the pails, the work surfaces, and finally the stables as well, throwing open the windows and sluicing the dung into the gutters.

By this time it was noon. He would eat something and throw himself into bed for an hour, dreaming of grass that wouldn't grow, or of cows that would not give milk, or of milk that would not churn; then he'd get up with the thought of building an enclosure for the calves, or of digging a drainage ditch where the rains had waterlogged the pasture. At four the cows would be brought to the stable for the second milking. At seven Lara would take them back out again, and at that point she would take over; there was no more work to do, and life at the farmstead slowed down and eased into the calm of the evening.

That was when Bruno would tell me about these things. We would sit outside waiting for sunset, with a half-liter of wine to keep us company. We contemplated the sparse pastures on the mountain's reverse side, where we had once gone searching for goats. At twilight a breeze would begin to blow from further down the valley, immediately chilling the air by a few degrees, carrying a fragrance of moss and damp earth, together perhaps with that of a deer wandering at the margins of the wood. One of the dogs would catch its scent and abandon the herd to pursue it: only one of the two, and not always the same one—as if they had an agreement between them to take turns hunting and guarding. The cows were calm now.

The sound of the bells reached us more faintly, descending to their lower tones.

Bruno did not like to think about practical problems with me. He never talked to me about debts, bills, taxes, mortgage rates. He preferred to talk about his dreams, or about the sense of physical intimacy he felt when milking, or about the mystery of rennet.

"Rennet is a little piece of a calf's stomach," he explained. "Imagine: part of the stomach that enables the calf to digest its mother's milk; we take it and use it to make cheese. It's right to do so, don't you think? But it's also terrible. Without this piece of stomach, the cheese would not form."

"I wonder who first discovered that," I said.

"It must have been the wild man."

"The wild man?"

"For us he was an ancient man who lived in the woods. Long hair, beard, covered in leaves. Every so often he would go around the villages, and people feared him—but they still left something outside for him to eat, to thank him for having shown them how to use rennet."

"A man who resembled a tree?"

"Part man, part beast, part tree."

"And what's he called in dialect?"

"*Omo servadzo*."

It was nearly nine in the evening. In the pasture the cows were little more than shadows. Lara was a shadow too, wrapped in a woolen shawl. She was standing still, attending to the herd. If a cow strayed too far she would call her by name, and the dog would charge off to collect her, needing no command.

"Is there also a wild woman?" I asked.

Bruno understood what I was thinking. "She's really good," he said. "She's strong and never gets tired. You know what I don't like? Not having the time to be together as much as I want. There's too much work. I get up at four in the morning, and in the evening start nodding off at the table."

"Love is for the winter," I said.

Bruno laughed. "That's so true. Not many mountain folk are born in spring. We're all born in autumn, like the calves."

It was the only allusion to sex that I had ever heard him make. "So when are you getting married?" I asked.

"Ah, if it was up to me then right away. She's the one who doesn't want to hear anything about marriage. Not in church, or at the registry, or anywhere else for that matter. It's those city ways of yours; go figure."

We were finishing the wine. Then we got up to go to the stable before it was completely dark. Lara was bringing back the herd with the help of one of the dogs, and now the other one also appeared from somewhere, returning to duty at the sound of the cowbells. Without any hurry the cows formed a line that came down through the pasture and stopped at the drinking trough. In the stable each one found its proper position for the night, while Bruno chained up their collars and I tied their tails to a rope, strung high so that they would not get too dirty when they lay down. There was a knot that I had learned to tie with a quick twist of the fingers. We would close the door and go to eat while the cows began to ruminate in the darkness.

• • •

Later on I would go back to Barma by the light of a torch. There was room at the farmstead, and Bruno and Lara always invited me to stay, but something pushed me to say goodbye to them and to take the path for the lake. It was as if I were seeking a proper distance from that fledgling family, and that leaving was a way of respecting them, and of protecting myself.

What I had to protect in myself was my ability to live alone. It had taken time to get used to solitude, to turn it into a place that I could adjust myself to and feel good in; and yet I felt that the relationship between us was always a difficult one. And so I would head back towards the house as if to reestablish our understanding. If the sky was not overcast I would soon switch off the head torch. I needed no more than a quarter-moon, and the stars, to make my way along the path between the larch trees. Nothing was stirring at that hour, only my footfall and the river that continued to splash and gurgle as the wood slept. In the silence its voice was clearest, and I could make out the sound peculiar to each bend, rapid, waterfall—muffled by the vegetation, then becoming gradually sharper over scree.

Higher up even the river went quiet. This was the point at which it disappeared beneath the rocks and ran underground. I began to hear a much lower sound, of the wind that was blowing in the basin. The lake was a nocturnal sky in motion; the wind was pushing flurries of small waves from one side to another, and as it changed direction it extinguished and rekindled along its lines of force the gleams of stars reflected in the black water. I stood still, watching these patterns. It seemed to me to recall the life of the mountain before mankind. I did not disturb it; I was a welcome guest. I realized again that in this company I would never be alone.

• • •

One morning towards the end of July I went down to the village with Lara. I was heading back to Turin for a while; she was taking down the first batch of cheese which had matured for six weeks. There was a mule that Bruno had acquired for the job: not the gray male that I'd used years ago to transport the cement, but a female with a thick, dark coat; smaller and more suited to the life of the farmstead. He had made a wooden packsaddle, on which he had stacked twelve loaves of cheese, sixty kilos in total, the first precious load that was being dispatched to the valley.

It was a momentous event for him, and for us. After securing the load he gave a kiss to Lara, a pat on the flank to the mule, and nodded in my direction, saying: "Berio, you know the way." He said goodbye to us and went to clean the stable. Just as on the building site he had decided that transportation was no kind of work for him: the mountain man stayed in the mountains, the mountain man's woman went up and down with things. He would not go down until the time came to leave the farmstead for the winter.

We started out on the path in single file, myself in front and Lara behind with the mule—and behind them one of the dogs who followed her everywhere. At first the mule advanced unsteadily, adjusting herself to the load. With her you had to proceed more carefully going down than when climbing back up, because the packsaddle unbalanced her with its weight bearing forwards on her front legs, and you needed to help her on the steepest slopes by holding firm to the rope tied around her neck. Further down, at the bottom of the pasture, the path crossed the river and flattened out. It was the spot where I had watched Bruno disappear on his motorbike, before losing sight of him altogether for all those years. From here on Lara and I were able to walk side by side, with the dog going in and out of the wood hunting for game, and the mule following just behind us, her breathing and the sound made by her shod hooves becoming a calm presence at our backs.

"What does he mean when he calls you that?" asked Lara.

"Calls me what?"

"Berio."

"Ah, he wants to remind me of something, I think. It was the name he gave me when I was a boy."

"And what are you meant to remember?"

"The road. Jesus, how many times I've gone up and down it. In August I would come up from Grana every day, and he would leave the pasture to bunk off with me. Then he'd take quite a beating from his uncle, but he couldn't care less. Twenty years ago. And now here we are carrying down his cheese. Everything has changed, and yet everything is the same."

"What has changed most?"

"The farmstead for sure. And the river. It was very different then. Did you know that we used to play down there?"

"Yes," Lara said. "The river game."

I kept quiet for a while. Thinking about the path had brought to mind that first time with my father, when we'd gone to meet Bruno's uncle. And as Lara and I descended I thought I saw coming out of the past a young boy walking in front of his father. The father was wearing a red jumper and plus fours, puffing like a bellows and spurring his son on. Good day to you! I imagined myself saying to him. The boy sure can run, eh! Who knows whether my father would have stopped to greet this man who was coming down from the future with a girl, a mule, a dog, and a load of cheese.

"Bruno's a bit worried about you," Lara said.

"About me?"

"He says that you're always alone. He thinks that you're not well."

I began to laugh. "Is that what you two talk about?"

"Every so often."

"And what do you think?"

"I don't know."

She thought about it and then gave a different answer: "That it's your choice. That sooner or later you'll get tired of being on your own, and that you'll find somebody. But you've chosen to live like this, so that's fine."

"That's right," I said.

And then, to make light of it, I added: "And do you know what he's told me? That he's asked you to marry him but that you won't hear of it."

"That lunatic?" she replied, laughing. "Never in a million years!"

"Why not?"

"Who would want to get married to someone who never wants to come down from the mountain? Someone who has spent all that he has in order to stay up there and make cheese?"

"Is it as bad as all that?"

"See for yourself. We've been working for a month and a half, and this is all we have to show for it," she said, pointing to what was behind us.

She became serious. For a good while she remained silent, thinking about what troubled her. We were almost there when she said "I like what we're doing, a lot. Even when it rains all day and I'm out in it pasturing the cows. It makes me very calm, makes me feel that I can think clearly about things, and that many of them no longer have any importance. For someone thinking about the money, it's lunacy. But I don't want any other life now. I want this one."

There was a small white van in the piazza in Grana, next to a tractor, a cement mixer, and my own car that had been parked there for a month. Two workers were digging a ditch next to the road. A man who I had never seen before was waiting for us: he was around fifty, and there was nothing out of the ordinary about the scene, except for the strangeness to us of seeing cars, asphalt, and clean clothes after all those days spent with livestock.

I helped Lara unload the *toma* from the packsaddle, and the man inspected them one by one: feeling the crust, sniffing it, giving it a few taps with his knuckles to see if there were air bubbles inside. He seemed satisfied. In the van he had a set of scales, and as he loaded the cheeses he weighed them, noting down the weight in a ledger and a figure on a receipt which he handed to Lara. At the bottom of it their first earnings were recorded. I watched her face as she looked at that number, but got no hint of her reaction to it. She said goodbye to me through the window of my car, then took the path again with the mule and the dog. They disappeared into the wood, or the wood reclaimed them as its own.

• • •

In Turin I vacated the apartment that I'd lived in for the last ten years. It was no longer worth keeping, given how little I used it, but on leaving I experienced a certain melancholy. I remembered vividly what it had meant to go there to live, when the city seemed so full of promises for the future. I didn't know now whether they had been just an illusion of mine, or whether the city itself had failed to keep them, but to empty in one day a home made over so many years, taking out jumbled-together things that had been brought there one by one, was like taking back an engagement ring, resigning oneself to defeat.

For a nominal rent a friend was letting me a room for my stays in Turin. I loaded other boxes of my things into the car and took them to my mother's place in Milan. From the motorway Monte Rosa emerged above the haze like a mirage: in the city the heat was melting the asphalt, and it seemed to me that I was pointlessly shifting stuff from one place to another, going up and down stairs of apartment buildings expiating who knows what sin that I'd committed in the past.

My mother was in Grana during this period, so I spent more than a month alone in the old apartment, by day doing the rounds of the offices of the producers I was working with, and at night watching the traffic from the window, imagining the anemic river buried beneath the avenue. There was nothing that belonged to me, nothing that I felt I belonged to. I was trying to get into production a series of documentaries on the Himalayas that would keep me away for a long time. It took a lot of fruitless meetings before finding someone who had faith in me: in the end I secured funding that would cover the cost of travel and not much else. But for me it was enough.

When I went back up to Grana in September there was a cold air blowing and a few chimneys in the village were smoking. Once out of the car I noticed a smell on my body that I did not like, so at the beginning of the path I washed my face and neck in the river; and in the woods rubbed my hands with a green larch twig. These were my usual rituals, but I knew that it would take a few days to be properly clean of the city.

All along the deep valley the pastures were beginning to fade. On Bruno's land, beyond the bridge of planks, the bank of the river was all trampled by the hooves of the herd: from there upwards the grass was finished, closely shaved and already fertilized, and there were patches of earth where the odd cow would scrape on days of bad weather, unsettled by the smell of a thunderstorm. I could smell a storm in the air right now, together with the pungent odor of dung and of wood smoke rising from Bruno's home. This was the time when he would be making the cheese, so I decided to head straight on and come down to find him on another occasion.

Having passed the stable, I heard the cowbells and saw Lara pasturing the herd high up, far from the path, on slopes where the last grass remained; I waved to her, and having already caught sight of me, she waved back with her unopened umbrella. The first drops of rain were beginning to fall, and after all those nights made restless by the heat and by dreams, I felt overcome by exhaustion: I just wanted to get to Barma, light the stove, and sleep. There was nothing like a long sleep in my burrow inside the mountain to put me right again.

There followed three days of fog during which I hardly left the house. I would stay at the window observing the way in which the clouds rose up from the valley and insinuated themselves into the woods, passing between the branches of the larch and fading the colors of my prayer flags before swallowing them completely. In the house the low pressure extinguished the fire in the stove, smoking me as I read or wrote. Then I would go out into the fog and stretch my legs by walking to the lake. There I would throw a stone that would vanish even before producing its phantom thud, and I imagined schools of small curious fish swimming around it. In the evening I would listen to some Swiss radio station or other, thinking about the year that was in store for me. It was a period of incubation, of the kind appropriate before great exploits.

On the third day there was a knock at the door. It was Bruno. He said: "So it is true that you're back. Want to come to the mountain?"

"Now?" I asked, since everything was shrouded in fog outside.

"Come on, I'll show you something."

"And the cows?"

"Let the cows be. It won't kill them."

And so we set off climbing back up the slope, along the path that led to the higher lake. Bruno was wearing his rubber boots, filthy with dung up to his thighs, and as we walked he told me that he had been into the slurry pit to pull out a cow that had fallen into it in the fog. He laughed. He was going up in a rush, so quickly that I was struggling to keep up. A viper had bitten one of the dogs, he said: he realized because he saw him next to water all the time, constantly thirsty, and checking him over had found the puncture marks made by the viper in his swollen belly. He was dragging himself around pitifully, and Lara was ready to put him on the mule and take him to the vet when Bruno's mother had said to give him as much milk as he would drink, just milk and no water or food—and now he had recovered and was gradually regaining his strength.

"With animals there is always something new to learn," he said. He shook his head and resumed climbing with that pace of his that nearly did for me. All the way up to the lake he continued talking about cows, milk, manure, grass, because during my absence so many things had happened that I needed to be informed about. He was thinking of bringing some rabbits and chickens up some time in the future, but he needed to build some good fences because there were foxes about. Eagles too. You might not believe it, but the eagle is even more ferocious than the fox when it comes to farmyard animals.

He didn't ask me how I had got on in Turin or in Milan. He wasn't interested in anything I might have been up to during the course of a whole month. He talked about foxes and eagles and rabbits and chickens, and pretended, as usual, that the city didn't exist and that I didn't have another life elsewhere: our friendship existed there, on that mountain, and what happened down below should not even be mentioned.

"And the business, how's that going?" I asked, as we got our breath back at the small lake.

Bruno shrugged his shoulders. "Well," he said.

"Are the sums adding up?"

He grimaced. He looked at me as if I had asked an annoying question, just for the pleasure of ruining his day. Then he said: "I leave the accounts to Lara. I've tried doing them myself, but I guess I'm no good at it."

We climbed up the scree in thick fog, with no path, each of us finding his own way. We couldn't see well enough to follow the cairns, losing sight of them almost immediately in fact, and letting ourselves be guided by the incline, our instincts, the lines suggested by the scree itself. We were climbing up blind, and every so often I heard the sound of stones that Bruno had dislodged above or below me, made out his outline and headed straight towards it. If we got too far from each other, one of us would call out: *oh?* and the other would respond with *oh!* We adjusted our direction like two boats in fog.

Until, at a certain point, I realized that the light was changing. Now it was casting shadows on the rocks in front of me. I looked up and saw a blue tone in the flurries of increasingly sparse fog, and after a few more steps I was through it: all at once I found myself looking around in full sunlight, with a September sky above my head and the dense white of the clouds beneath my feet. We were well above two and a half thousand meters. Only a few peaks emerged at that height, like chains of islands, like surfacing dorsals.

I also saw that we had deviated from the proper route to the Grenon's summit, or at least from the usual one: but instead of crossing the scree at the fork I decided to reach the crest by climbing what was immediately above me. It didn't look difficult. As I climbed I fantasized about achieving a first, something that would be recorded in the annals of the Italian Alpine Club, together with the author of such a feat: *North-west crest of the Grenon: Pietro Guasti, 2008*. But just a little further up, on a ledge, I found a few rusty meat or sardine tins of the kind that many years ago no one bothered to take back with them to the valley. So I discovered once again that someone had preceded me.

There was a gorge between where I was and the usual route, getting steeper and steeper up to the crest. Bruno had taken it, and on its steep slope I saw that he had developed a peculiar style of his own: he used his hands as well and climbed on all fours, rapidly, instinctively choosing the right places for his hands and feet, and never putting his whole weight on them. Sometimes the ground would give way beneath his feet or hands, but his momentum had already carried him forward, and the small cascades of stones that he dislodged continued on down, like memories of his passing through there. *Omo servadzo*: the wild man, I thought. Having got to the top before him, I had time to admire this new style of his from the crest.

"Who taught you to climb like that?" I asked.

"The chamois. I watched them once and said to myself: now I'm going to try it like that too."

"And it works?"

"Well . . . I've still got a few improvements to make."

"Did you know that we would get above the clouds?"

"I was hoping that we would."

We sat down, leaning against the pile of stones where I had once found words written by my father. The sun was sculpting every edge and indentation in the rock, and doing the same to Bruno's face: he had new crow's feet around his eyes, shadows under his cheekbones, furrows that I did not recall him having before. His first season at the farmstead must have been hard going.

It seemed like the right moment to talk to him about my journey. I told him that in Milan I had secured enough funding to stay away for at least a year. I wanted to go around the regions of Nepal and portray the people that lived in its mountains: there were so many different groups in the valleys of the Himalayas, all distinct from each other. I would be leaving in October, near the end of the monsoon season. I had little money but many contacts—people working there who would be able to help me and put me up. I confided that I had given up my home in Turin, that I didn't have another one there now and neither did I want one: if things went well in Nepal, I would stay there even longer.

Bruno listened in silence. When I had finished speaking he took a while to reflect on the implications of what I had told him. He was looking at Monte Rosa, and said: "Do you remember that time with your father?"

"Of course I remember."

"I think about it sometimes, you know? Do you think the ice of that day has reached the bottom yet?"

"I don't think so. It's probably about halfway."

Then he asked: "Are the Himalayas like our region at all?"

"No," I replied. "Not at all."

It was not easy to explain, but I wanted to try, and so I added: "You know those enormous ruined monuments, like the ones in

Athens and Rome? Those ancient temples of which only a few columns are left standing, with the stones of their walls lying scattered about on the ground? Well, the Himalayas are like the original temple. It's like being able to see it intact after having spent a lifetime only ever seeing ruins."

I immediately regretted having spoken in this way. Bruno was gazing at the glaciers, above the clouds, and I thought that in the coming months I would remember him like this, like the custodian of that pile of rubble.

Then he got up. "Time to do the milking," he said. "Are you coming down?"

"I think I'll stay here a bit longer."

"Good for you. Who would want to go back down below?"

He entered the gorge up which he'd climbed and disappeared amongst the rocks. I caught sight of him again a few minutes later, about a hundred meters further down. There was a spit of snow down there, pushed northwards, and he had crossed the scree in order to reach it. From above that small snowfield he tested its consistency with his foot. He looked up in my direction and waved, and I responded with a big gesture that might be seen from a distance. The snow must have been well frozen, because Bruno jumped on it and immediately picked up speed: he went down with his legs spread out, skiing with his work boots, waving his arms to keep his balance—and in an instant was swallowed up by the fog.

ELEVEN

ANITA WAS BORN in the autumn, like all mountain folk.

I was not there that year: in Nepal I had come into contact with the world of NGOs and was working with a group of them. I was filming documentaries in the villages where schools and hospitals were being built, agricultural projects or employment initiatives for women were being developed, and where sometimes camps for Tibetan refugees were being set up. I didn't like everything that I was seeing. The managers in Kathmandu were no more than careerist politicians. But in the mountains themselves I came across people of every sort: from old hippies to students doing VSO; from volunteer medics to mountaineers who between one expedition and another would stay on to work as builders. Not even these examples of humanity were entirely free from ambition and power struggles, but what they did not lack was idealism. And I liked being amongst idealists.

I was in Mustang, in June—an arid plateau on the border with Tibet, made up of small white houses clinging to the red rock—when my mother wrote to let me know that she had just gone up to Grana and discovered that Lara was five months pregnant. She felt immediately called to do her duty. Throughout the summer she sent me updates that resembled medical reports: in June Lara had twisted her ankle while she was out in the pasture, and had continued to hobble around for days; in July, with her very pale skin, she suffered sunstroke while making hay; in August, with backache and swollen legs, she still carried down the cheese twice a week with the mule. My mother would order her to rest. Lara would not hear of it. When Bruno suggested that they should hire someone to do her work she refused, saying that the cows were all pregnant too and that no one made a fuss about it, that seeing them so calm actually helped her to relax.

I had come to Kathmandu at the height of the monsoon season. Every afternoon the city was whipped by a storm. Then the crazy traffic of motorbikes and bicycles would cease, the packs of street dogs would seek refuge under overhanging roofs, the streets themselves become rivers of mud and rubbish—and I would shut myself in some place or other with a phone line, in front of an ancient computer, and catch up on the latest news. I did not know whether to admire Lara most, expecting her first child in an *alpeggio*, or that other woman, now seventy years old, who would climb up to visit her on foot and accompany her to the hospital each month. The August scan established beyond doubt that Lara was expecting a girl. Even now she continued to pasture the cows, with a belly so big that it prevented any movement except simply walking in front of the herd, then sitting under a tree to watch over it.

Then on the last Sunday of September, with their hides brushed and shining, their embroidered leather collars and their ceremonial bells, the cows went down to the valley in a solemn end of season procession. Bruno installed them in the stable he had rented for the winter, and at that point there was nothing left to do but wait. He must have done a certain amount of calculation, in true mountain man style, because Lara gave birth soon after, as if that too was seasonal work.

I remember where I was when my mother gave me the news: in lower Dolpo, on the shore of a lake that uncannily resembled an Alpine one, surrounded by woods of red fir and Buddhist temples, together with a girl that I had met in Kathmandu. She worked at an orphanage in the city, but at that time we had taken a few days off and headed for the mountains together. In a refuge without a stove at three and a half thousand meters, the walls of which were nothing more than small shingles painted blue, we had put together our two sleeping bags and huddled inside: through the window I looked out at the star-studded sky and the pointed tops of the fir trees as she slept. At a certain point I saw the moon rise. I stayed awake a long time, thinking about my friend Bruno who had just become a father.

• • •

When I returned to Italy in 2010 I found it deep in a grotesque economic crisis. Milan announced it to me on arrival, with its airport looking virtually decommissioned: four planes on kilometers of runway, and the window displays of the high fashion brands glistening in the empty shops. From the train that took me to the city, freezing from the air conditioning on a July evening, I noticed building sites everywhere, tall cranes suspended, high-rise buildings with bizarre profiles that were taking shape on the horizon. I could not understand why all the newspapers were talking about all the money having run out when I was noticing in Milan, and also in Turin, a building boom that resembled that of a golden age. Going in search of old friends was like doing a tour of hospital wards: the production companies, the advertising agencies, and the television channels that I had worked for were shutting down due to bankruptcy, and many of those friends were at home on their sofas, doing nothing. Nearing forty, they were reduced to taking the odd day's work and to accepting money from their retired parents. But look outside, one of them said to me, do you see the buildings sprouting up everywhere? Who is it that's stealing what was due to us? Wherever I went I breathed in this air of disillusionment and anger, this intergenerational sense of grievance. It was a relief to have in my pocket already the ticket with which I would be able to leave.

A few days later I took a coach to the mountains, then another at the beginning of the valley, and got off at the bar where I used to go with my mother to make calls, though there was no longer any trace there of the red phone box.

I followed the path on foot, just as before. The old mule track cut through the bends of the asphalted road and soon became choked with brambles and leaves, so rather than follow it I went up through the woods, relying on my memory of the way. When I came out on the other side I discovered that next to the ruins of the tower a mobile phone mast had gone up, and that down in the gully a cement dam interrupted the flow of the river. The little artificial reservoir was full of mud from the thaw: an excavator was fishing it out of the water and dumping it on the bank, destroying with its caterpillar tracks and the muddy sand the meadows where Bruno used to graze cattle as a boy.

Then, as always, I got beyond Grana and it seemed like I was leaving every poisoned thing behind me. It was like entering the sacred valley when going to Annapurna: except that here it was not any religious precept but simply neglect that had left everything unchanged. I discovered again the clearing that as children Bruno and I called *the sawmill*, because two tracks remained there together with a trolley used who knows how long ago for cutting planks of wood for buildings. Nearby there was a cable lift for dispatching those planks up to the *alpeggi*, the steel cable wound around a larch tree that with the passage of time had engulfed it in bark. They had forgotten my childhood mountain because it wasn't worth anything—and it was fortunate in this respect. I slowed down like the Nepalese porters who would whisper at high altitude: *bistare, bistare.* I did not want these moments to be over too soon. Every time

I went back up there I felt like I was returning to my own self, to the place where I was most like myself again and felt best.

At the farmstead they were expecting me for lunch. Bruno, Lara, the little Anita who at less than a year old was playing on a blanket in the middle of a meadow, and my mother who did not take her eyes off her for a moment. She said: "It's your Uncle Pietro, Anita, look!" and immediately brought her to me to get acquainted. The little girl looked at me with suspicion, intrigued by my beard; she tugged it, and making a sound that I didn't catch started laughing at her new discovery. My mother seemed quite different from the aging woman I had said goodbye to when I left. Other things had altered too; the whole farmstead was livelier than I remembered it: the new chickens and rabbits, the mule, the cows, the dogs, a fire on which the polenta and a stew were cooking, the table laid in the open air.

Bruno was so pleased to see me again that he embraced me. It was a gesture so unusual between us that as he squeezed me I wondered how much he might have changed. When we separated I looked hard at his face, searching for wrinkles, gray hairs, the heaviness of age in his features. I had the impression that he was looking for the same in mine. Were we still the same? Then he sat me down at the head of the table and poured the drinks: four glasses brimming with red wine with which to toast my return.

I was no longer used to wine or meat, and soon felt intoxicated by both. I was speaking nonstop. Lara and my mother took turns to get up and look after Anita, until the little girl began to feel sleepy and there was a sign, I think, or a silent understanding between them, and my mother gathered her up in her arms and moved away cradling her. I had brought back as a gift a teapot, cups, and a packet of black tea, so after lunch I made some, Tibetan style, with butter and salt, even if the Alpine butter was not as strong or rancid as butter made from yak's milk. While I was mixing it I told them that in Tibet they used butter in every way imaginable: they burned it in lamps, spread it as a moisturizer on women's hair, mixed it with human bones in sky burials.

"What?" said Bruno.

I explained that on the high plateaus there wasn't enough wood to cremate corpses: the dead were flayed and left on top of a hill so that the vultures would devour them. After a few days they would return and find the bones picked clean. The skull and the skeleton were then pounded up and mixed with butter and flour, so that this too would become food for the birds.

"How horrible," Lara said.

"But why?" said Bruno.

"Can you imagine it? The dead person there on the ground and the vultures eating them piece by piece?"

"Well, being put in a hole in the ground is not so very different," I said. "Something will end up eating you there as well."

"Yes, but at least you don't have to see it," Lara said.

"I think it's a great idea," said Bruno. "Food for the birds."

On the other hand he was disgusted by the tea, and emptied our cups as well as his own before filling them with grappa instead. The three of us were all a little drunk by now. He put his arm around Lara's shoulders and said: "And what about the Himalayan girls? Are they as beautiful as those in the Alps?"

I became serious without meaning to and mumbled something in reply.

"You're not turning into some kind of Buddhist monk, are you?"

But Lara had picked up on the meaning of my reticence, and answered for me: "No, no. There is someone who is keeping him company."

Then Bruno looked at my face and smiled, seeing there that it was true, and I instinctively looked over to where my mother was, too far off to hear what we were saying.

Later on I went to lie down beneath an old larch, a solitary tree that dominated the meadows above the house. I remained stretched out there with my eyes half-closed and my hands behind my head, looking at the summits and the ridges of the Grenon through the branches and surrendering to sleep. That view always reminded me of my father. I thought that in some way, without knowing it, this strange family amongst which I had found myself had been founded by him. Who knows what he would have made of it, seeing us all together at that lunch. His wife, his son, his other son from the mountains, a young woman, and a little girl. If we had really been brothers, I thought, Bruno could be nothing other than the eldest. He was the one who made things. The builder of houses, a family, a business: the firstborn with his land, his livestock, his offspring. I was the younger brother, the squanderer. The one who does not get married, does not have children, and who travels the world without sending news for months at a time, turning up out of the blue on the day of a party, just as lunch is about to be served. Who would have thought that, eh Dad? Immersed in these alcohol-induced musings, I fell asleep in the sun.

• • •

I spent a few weeks with them that summer. Not long enough to stop feeling that I was only visiting, but too long to just sit around doing nothing. Up at Barma my two-year absence had left its mark, so much so in fact that when I saw the house again I felt like apologizing: the invasive vegetation had already begun to lay siege to her, certain roof tiles were warped or out of place, and when I left I had forgotten to remove the piece of chimney flue that stuck out of the wall, so that the snow had broken it and caused some damage inside the house as well. It would have taken only a few more years for the mountain to reclaim her, and to reduce her again to the pile of rubble that she was before. I decided to devote my remaining time there to the house, preparing her for my next departure.

Spending time with Bruno and Lara I discovered that something else had begun to deteriorate while I was away. When my mother was not there and Anita had been put to bed, the place changed from being a happy farmstead to being a business that was in the red—and my friends became squabbling financial partners. Lara talked about nothing else. She told me that the sums they made from cheese making did not even cover the mortgage repayments. The money came and went, leaving them with nothing to spare, and making no inroad on their debt with the bank. Living up there in the summer they were able to be almost self-sufficient, but in the winter, what with the rent for the stables and other costs, they were really struggling. They had needed to take out another loan. New debts with which to pay for old.

That summer Lara had decided to cut out the middleman, bypassing the distributor that I had met and selling directly to shopkeepers, even though it meant a load more work for her. Twice every week she would leave the little girl with my mother in Grana and go by car to make deliveries, leaving Bruno to manage on his own. They should have taken someone on, but this would have put them back where they started again.

He would start fuming soon after she began telling me about these things. One evening he said: "Can't we change the subject? We hardly ever see Pietro. Do we always have to be talking about money?"

Lara took offense. "So what should we be talking about?" she said. "Let's see, what about yaks? What do you think, Pietro, could we set up a nice business breeding yaks?"

"It's not such a bad idea," Bruno said.

"Listen to him," Lara said to me. "Living up here on the mountain with his head in the clouds he doesn't have any of the problems of us mere mortals. And then to him— But remember that it's you who got us into this mess, right?"

"That's right," said Bruno. "They're my debts. You shouldn't take them too much to heart."

Hearing that she glared at him furiously, got up abruptly, and left. He immediately regretted having uttered such words.

"She's right," he said. "But what can I do? I can't work any harder than I am already. And thinking about money all the time solves nothing, so it's preferable to think about something else, isn't it?"

"But how much do you need?" I asked.

"Forget it. If I told you you'd be shocked."

"Perhaps I can help. Perhaps I can stay here and work until the end of the season."

"Thanks, but no."

"You wouldn't have to pay me of course. I'd be only too pleased to help."

"No," said Bruno, curtly.

• • •

In the days that were left before my departure we did not mention the subject again. Lara kept to herself, offended, worried, busying herself around the little girl. Bruno pretended that nothing had happened. I would go up and down from Grana with the materials I needed to fix the house: I had reapplied cement where it was needed, stopped up the chimney flue, cleared the weeds from the surrounding land. I'd had larch tiles cut similar to the old ones, and was on the roof replacing them when Bruno arrived to see me: perhaps he had intended us to go up the mountain together, but finding me on the roof changed his mind, and he climbed up to join me there instead.

It was a job that we had already done, six years ago now. We quickly found our old rhythm. Bruno removed the old nails and I threw them down onto the grass, then I put the new tile into place and held it firm while he hammered it down. There was no need to say anything. For an hour it seemed as if we had gone back to that summer, when our lives still had direction and we had nothing to worry about other than building a wall or raising a beam. It was over too quickly. In the end the roof was like new, and I went to the fountain to get two beers that I kept cold there in its icy water.

That morning I had taken down the prayer flags, faded by the sun and rain and torn by the wind, and had burned them in the stove. Then I hung up some new ones, stringing them this time between the rock face and a corner of the house rather than between trees, thinking about the stupas that I had seen in Nepal. Now they were dancing in the wind above my father's epitaph, seeming to be blessing him. Bruno was watching them when I went back onto the roof.

"What's written on those things?" he asked.

"They're prayers asking for good fortune," I said. "Prosperity. Peace. Harmony."

"And do you believe in that?"

"In what, good fortune?"

"No, in praying."

"I don't know. But they put me in a good mood. And that's enough, no?"

"Yes, you're right."

I was reminded of our own good luck charm, and looked to see how it was getting on. The little Swiss pine was still there, as delicate and contorted as the day when it was transplanted—but still alive. By now it was heading towards its seventh winter. It too was swaying in the wind, but inspired neither peace nor harmony: tenacity, if anything. A clinging on to life. I thought that in Nepal these were not virtues—but that in the Alps, perhaps, they were.

I opened the beers. Handing one to Bruno I asked: "So how's it going, being a father?"

"How's it going? I'd like to know the answer to that myself."

He raised his eyes to the sky, and then added: "For now it's easy.

I carry her in my arms and stroke her as if she were a little rabbit or a kitten. That I know how to do. I've always done it. The difficulty will come when I have to tell her about things."

"But why?"

"What do I know about anything? In my life I've only ever known this."

When he said *this* he made a gesture with his hand to encompass the lake, the woods, the meadows, and the scree that we had in front of us. I did not know if he had ever gone away from there, or if he had, how far. I had never even asked, partly in order not to offend him, partly because the answer would not have changed anything.

He said: "I know how to milk a cow, how to make cheese, to cut down a tree, to build a house. I would also know how to shoot an animal and eat it if I was starving. I've been taught these things since I was little. But who teaches you how to be a father? Not my own father, that's for sure. In the end I had to beat him up so that he would leave me alone. Have I ever told you about that?"

"No," I said.

"Well, that's what happened. I was working all day on the building site; I was stronger than him. I think I must have really hurt him because I haven't seen him since. The poor bastard."

He looked up at the sky again. The same wind that was agitating my prayer flags was pushing the clouds over the ridges. He said: "I'm only glad that Anita's a girl, so I can just love her and that's that."

I had never seen him so low. Things had not gone as he had hoped. I had the same sense of powerlessness as when we were boys and he would not utter a word for an entire day, plunged into a despondency that seemed absolute and irremediable. I would like to have had some old friend's trick with which to raise his spirits.

Before he left, the legend of the eight mountains came to my mind, and I thought that he might like to hear it. Relating it to him I tried to remember every word and gesture with which the chicken carrier had given it to me. With a nail I scratched the mandala on a wooden tile.

"So you're supposed to be the one who journeys to the eight mountains, and I'm the one who climbs Sumeru?"

"It looks like it."

"And which one of us achieves something good?"

"It's you," I said. Not just to encourage him, but because I believed it.

Bruno said nothing. He looked at the drawing again, in order to memorize it. Then he gave me a pat on the back and jumped down from the roof.

• • •

Without having in any way planned it, I too found myself caring for children in Nepal. Not in the mountains but on the periphery of Kathmandu, a city that now sprawled across its entire valley with outskirts resembling the shanty towns to be found in so many other parts of the world. They were the children of people who had come to the city seeking their fortune. Some had lost one of their parents, some had lost both, but more often than not the father or mother lived in a shack and worked like a slave in that ants' nest, leaving them to be raised on the streets. These children had been dealt a fate that did not exist in the mountains: in Kathmandu the child beggars, the small gangs dedicated to some kind of trafficking or other, and the dirty stupefied kids who scavenged through the city's rubbish were as familiar a part of the urban landscape as street dogs and the monkeys in the Buddhist temples.

There were organizations that were trying to care for them, and the girl I was with was working for one of these. Given what I was seeing for myself on the streets, and hearing about from her, it was inevitable that I would begin to lend a hand too. You find your place in the world much less predictably than you'd imagine: here I was, after so much wandering, in a big city at the foot of the mountains, with a woman who was basically doing the same work as my mother did. And with whom, at every opportunity, I would escape to altitude in order to replenish the energy sapped by the city.

Walking these paths I thought often about Bruno. It wasn't the woods or the rivers so much as the children that reminded me of him. I remembered him at their age, growing up in what remained of his dying village, with ruins as his only playground and a school that had been turned into a storehouse. There was a lot to be doing in Nepal, for someone with his skills: we taught the migrant children English and maths from textbooks, but perhaps what we should have been showing them was how to cultivate a plot, how to build a stable, raise goats—and so I would sometimes fantasize about dragging Bruno away from his dying mountain, to help teach these other mountain folk. We could have done great things together in this part of the world.

And yet if it had just been down to us we would not have contacted each other for years, as though our friendship had no need of being kept up. It was my mother who gave us news of each other, since she was all too familiar with living with men who did not communicate amongst themselves. She wrote to me about Anita, about the character that she was developing, about the way in which she was growing up wild and fearless. She had become very attached to this little girl, and it worried her to see the crisis between her parents worsening. They worked too hard, and continued to find ways of working even harder: so much so that in the summer my mother would frequently keep Anita with her at Grana, in order to free her parents from at least the burden of having to care for her too. Lara was exasperated by their debts. Bruno had retreated into mutism and into his work. My mother did not mention directly what she feared, but it was not difficult to read between the lines: we had both begun to see how things would end up.

They struggled on in this way for a little longer. Then in the autumn of 2013 Bruno declared himself bankrupt, shut down the agricultural business, and handed over the keys of the farm to the bailiff, and Lara went to live with her parents with the child. Although according to my mother, things had happened the other way round: Lara had decided to leave him, and he had given up, resigning himself to failure. Either way, it made no difference. But the tone in which she conveyed the news was not just sad but alarmed, and I could tell that she was afraid for what might happen to Bruno now. *He's lost everything,* she wrote, *and he is all alone. Is there anything you can do?*

I read these words several times before doing something that I had never done before in Nepal: I got up from the computer, asked to use the telephone, and went into a booth to dial the code for Italy and then Bruno's number. It was one of those places in Kathmandu where people seem permanently to be killing time. The owner was eating rice and lentils, an old man sitting next to him was watching him eat, and two children were peering into the booth at me to see what I was up to. The phone rang five or six times, at which point I began to think that Bruno would not answer it: knowing him, he might have hurled the mobile into the woods and decided not to hear from anyone ever again. Instead there was a click, a distant fumbling, and an uncertain voice that was saying:

"Hello?"

"Bruno!" I shouted. "It's me, Pietro!"

On hearing my outburst of Italian the boys burst out laughing. I pressed the receiver closer to my ear. The delay on the long-distance line added an extra hesitation, then Bruno said: "Yes, I'd hoped it would be you."

He did not feel like talking about what had happened with Lara. I could imagine anyway how it had been. I asked him how he was, and what he planned to do.

He replied: "I'm fine. I'm just tired. They took away the farm, did you hear?"

"Yes. And what did you do with the cows?"

"Oh, I gave them away."

"And what about Anita?"

"Anita is with Lara at her parents'. They've got plenty of room there. I've heard from them, they're doing fine."

Then he added: "Listen, I wanted to ask you something."

"Tell me."

"If I can use the house up at Barma, since at the moment I don't really know where to go."

"But do you really want to go up there?"

"I don't want to see anyone; you know how it is. I'll spend some time in the mountains."

That's how he said it: *in the mountains*. It was strange to hear his voice on a phone, in Kathmandu, a voice that arrived there hoarse and so distorted that I struggled to recognize it, but that I knew at that moment was really his. It was Bruno, my old friend.

I said: "Of course. Stay as long as you want. It's your house."

"Thanks."

There was something else I wanted to say, but it was difficult. We were not used to asking each other for help, or to offering it. Without beating around the bush I asked: "Listen, would you like me to come over?"

In the past Bruno would have immediately told me to stay where I was. When he eventually answered, he did so with a tone of voice that I had never heard before. Ironic, in part. And partly disarmed.

He said: "Well, that would be nice."

"I'll sort a few things out and then come, all right?"

"All right."

It was a late afternoon in November. As I left the place from which I'd phoned, darkness was falling over the city. In that part of the world the streets are not lit, and at sunset people hurry home, and you sense an anxiety about night falling. Outside there were dogs, dust, scooters, a cow lying in the middle of the road stopping the traffic, tourists heading for restaurants and hotels, the air of an evening in late summer. In Grana it was the beginning of winter, and it occurred to me that I had never before seen that season there.

TWELVE

THE DEEP-CUT VALLEY of Grana in October was burnt by drought and frost. It had the color of ochre, of sand, of terra-cotta, and looked as if its meadows had been burnt in a fire now spent. In its woods that fire was still ablaze: on the flanks of the mountain the gold and bronze flames of the larches were lit against the dark green of the pines, and raising your eyes to the sky warmed the soul. The sun no longer reached the bottom of the valley, and the earth was hard underfoot, covered here and there with a crust of frost. At the little wooden bridge, when I bent down to drink, I saw that the autumn had cast a spell over that river of mine: the ice was forming slides and galleries, draping the wet stones with glass, trapping tufts of dry grass and transforming them into found sculptures.

Climbing towards Bruno's farmstead I crossed paths with a group of hunters. They were wearing camouflage jackets and binoculars around their necks but had no rifles. They did not seem like locals to me, but then perhaps in the autumn even faces change, and I was the outsider here. They were talking together in dialect, and when they saw me they stopped talking, sized me up with a glance, and continued on their way. I found out soon after where they had stationed themselves: up at the farmstead, near the bench where Bruno and I would sit of an evening, I found their cigarette butts and a crumpled empty packet. They must have climbed up early in the morning in order to study the woods from that vantage point. Bruno had put everything in good order before leaving: he had sealed the stable door, closed the shutters, stacked the wood against the side of the house, overturned the drinking troughs along the wall. He had even spread the manure that was dry and odorless now in the yellowed meadows. It looked just like any other Alpine farmstead prepared for the winter months, and I lingered a while remembering how it was, full of noise and life, the last time that I had visited it. Breaking the silence I heard a belling from the other side of the valley. I had only ever heard this sound a few times before, but once would have been enough to remember it forever. It was the powerful, guttural, angry sound with which the stag intimidates his rivals in the mating season, even though it was too late now for reproduction. Perhaps the stag was just plain angry, nothing more. At this point I realized what those hunters had come looking for.

Something similar happened a little while later, up at the lake. The sun was just managing to peer over the crests of the Grenon, warming the scree facing it at midday. But the inlet at the foot of the slope remained in shadow even at this hour: a layer of ice had formed on the water, a half-moon that was polished and dark. When I tested it with a stick the ice was so thin that it broke. I took a piece of it from the water and held it up to look through, and at that moment I heard a chainsaw starting up. The revving of the motor, and then the squeal of the blade biting wood. I looked to see where it was coming from. There was a copse of larch midway up the slope, just above Barma, growing on a kind of small terrace: the naked, gray trunk of a dead tree stuck out amongst the yellow tresses of the others. I heard the chainsaw cutting into the wood, twice. Then the pause required to walk around the tree, then again the screech of the blade as it bit into the wood. I saw it slowly begin to topple before it suddenly collapsed, with a crackling rush of branches splitting as it fell.

• • •

"What can I tell you, Pietro, things went badly," Bruno said that evening, then shrugged his shoulders to indicate that he had nothing more to add on the subject. He was drinking coffee reheated on the stove and looking out to where it was getting dark already at five o'clock. We were using candles in the house, now that our little mill wheel was stopped due to drought: I had seen two full packs of white candles in the other room, together with the sacks of cornmeal, a couple of loaves of cheese remaining from the last batch made, a reserve of tins, some potatoes, and cartons of wine. It was not the larder of someone who was in any hurry to go back down. During the month since our phone call Bruno had laid in supplies and elaborated his own kind of mourning: the farm had gone badly, the relationship with Lara had gone badly, and he spoke about these things—or rather avoided speaking about them—as if they belonged to some remote period, in both time and thought. Rather than remember them, he seemed to want to forget about them entirely.

We spent these days making firewood for the winter. In the morning we would study a slope in search of a dead tree, climb up to cut it down, divest it of its branches before Bruno took off its top with the chainsaw, then would spend hours laboring to shift it to the house. We would tie a strong rope around it and drag it down by sheer force of our own strength. We had built slides throughout the wood, using old planks like sleepers, with banks of piled branches positioned where the trunk was in danger of slipping from our grasp with the steepness of the slope—but sooner or later it would get entangled with some obstacle or other, and then the work of dislodging it from there would begin. Bruno would curse it. He handled a pickaxe as if it were one of those small hoes lumberjacks use, levering up the trunk so that it could be pivoted halfway round: he would try one side and then the other, swearing as he did so, before flinging the tool to the ground and going to pick up the chainsaw again. I had always admired his way of working, the grace that he was able to express when using any kind of tool, but all trace of that was gone now. He would wield the chainsaw furiously: stall it, over-rev it, and when sometimes he had used up its petrol, would be on the verge of flinging it away as well. He would end up solving the problem by cutting the trunk into pieces and giving us another one instead—multiple journeys carrying them back to the house. Then we would set to splitting the wood with a sledgehammer and wedges until nightfall. The strokes of iron upon iron reverberated around the mountainside, drier, shriller, meaner, when Bruno was hammering, more uncertain and discordant when I took my turn. Until the master stroke came, the trunk split, and we finished the job with the axe.

The snow was already sparse on the Grenon. What little there was allowed the scree and the bushes, the ledges and the outcrops of rock to be made out still, as if the snowfall were no more than a thin layer of frost. But towards the end of the month a cold front arrived, the temperature dropped suddenly, and the lake froze over in the course of one night. The next morning I went down to look: the ice near the shore was rendered grayish and opaque by a myriad of trapped air bubbles, and became gradually darker and then blacker the further away you went from it. With a stick I could not even dent it, so decided to risk walking on it to see if it would take my weight. I had only taken a few steps before I heard a rumbling from deep in the lake that made me retreat immediately. Safely on the shore I heard it again: an ominous rumbling, resounding like a bass drum being hit over and over, extremely slowly and rhythmically, perhaps once every minute, perhaps even slower. It could not be anything other than water, beating against the ice from below. With the coming of daylight the water seemed to want to break out of the tomb in which it had found itself encased.

At sunset our endless evenings began. The horizon at the end of the valley would be tinged red for barely a few minutes before darkness fell. From then until it was time to sleep, the light did not change again: it could be six, seven, eight, and we would be spending the hours in front of the stove in silence, each with a candle to read by, the glow of the fire, the wine rationed to make it last, the one luxury at our suppers. During those days I cooked potatoes in every conceivable way. Boiled, roasted, grilled, fried in butter, baked with melted *toma*, with the candle next to the hotplate to see when they were done. We would eat them in ten minutes, then face each other for another two or three hours of silent vigil. The fact was that I was waiting for something—I didn't know what—something that wasn't happening. I had come back from Nepal to rescue my friend, and now my friend seemed to have no need of me. If I asked him a question he would let it drop with one of those vague responses that extinguished from the start any potential glimmer of conversation. He could spend an hour staring at the fire. And only occasionally, when I'd given up expecting him to, he spoke: but as if already midsentence, or as if he were temporarily following out loud the train of his own thoughts.

One evening he said, "I was there once, in Milan."

"Oh really?" I said.

"But it was a long time ago; I must have been twenty. One day I had an argument with my boss and walked off the site. I had a whole afternoon free, so I said to myself: right, I'll go there now. I took the car, went on the motorway, and arrived in the evening. I wanted to have a beer in Milan. I stopped at the first bar and had one. Then I headed back."

"And what did you think of Milan?"

"Not much. Too many people."

And then he added: "And I've also been to the sea. I went to Genoa once and saw it. I had a blanket in the car and slept there. Nobody was waiting for me at home anyway."

"And what was the sea like?"

"A big lake."

His accounts of things were like this; they might or might not have been true, and they went nowhere. Only once, out of the blue, he said: "It was great, wasn't it, when we used to sit in front of the stable in the evening?"

I put down the book I was reading and responded: "Yes, really great."

"The way night fell in July, the calm descended, do you remember? It was the hour I liked best, and then when I got up to milk the cows it was still dark. The two of them were still sleeping, and I felt as if I were watching over everything, as if they could sleep peacefully because I was there."

Then he added: "It's stupid, no? But that's how I felt."

"I don't see anything stupid about it."

"It's stupid because no one can look after anyone else. It's hard enough to look after yourself. Men are designed to always cope, if they're clever, but if they think they're too clever they end up being ruined."

"Is starting a family being too clever?"

"Perhaps it is, for some."

"Well, perhaps *some* should think twice before bringing children into the world."

"Yes, you're right," Bruno said.

I stared at him in the semidarkness, trying to understand what was going through his mind. One half of his face was yellowed by the light from the stove, the other completely dark.

"So what are you saying?" I asked. He stared at the fire as if I were no longer even there.

I felt an increasing impatience that drove me outside into the dark, craving a cigarette for company. I stayed outside looking for the stars that were not visible, and asking myself what I was doing back here, until I realized that my teeth were chattering. Then I went back into the warm, dark, smoky room. Bruno had not moved. I warmed my feet in front of the stove, then went up to shut myself into my sleeping bag.

The next morning I was the first to get up. In the light of day I did not feel like sharing that small room, so skipped coffee and went out for a walk. I went down to look at the lake and found it covered by an overnight frost that the wind was sweeping here and there—lifting it in flurries, puffs, and miniature whirlwinds that appeared and disappeared in an instant, like restless spirits. Beneath the frost the ice was black and looked like stone. As I stood there looking at it, a shot echoed in the valley, rebounding from one side to the other so that it was difficult to tell whether it came from below, in the woods, or from the crests above. But I instinctively looked upwards for its origin, scouring the scree and the slopes for any sign of movement.

When I got back to Barma I saw that two hunters had come to speak to Bruno. They had modern weapons with telescopic sights. At one point one of the two opened his rucksack and deposited a black bag at Bruno's feet. The other one noticed my presence and nodded in my direction, and recognizing something familiar about that gesture I realized soon enough who they were: the two cousins from whom Bruno had bought the farmstead. I had not seen them for more than twenty-five years. I had not known that he was in touch with them, nor how they had found him up there. But who knows how much else there was about Grana that I could not even imagine.

From out of the black bag, after they had gone, a dead and already gutted chamois emerged. When Bruno hung it up by its back legs from the branch of a larch tree I could see that it was a female. It had its dark winter coat with a thick black line down the middle of its back, a slender neck from which its lifeless muzzle dangled, two small horns that looked like hooks. From the gash in its belly the steam was still rising in the cold morning air.

Bruno went inside to fetch a knife and sharpened it carefully before setting to work. Then he was as precise and methodical as if he had spent a lifetime doing nothing but this. He made an incision in the skin around the shins and continued along the inside of the thighs, all the way down to the groin where the two cuts joined. He went back up, detached a flap of skin from the shin, put down the knife, and grasped the flap with both hands, tugging it down violently to expose first one thigh and then the other. Under the skin there was a white, viscous layer—the fat that the chamois had put on for the winter months—and beneath the fat you could glimpse the pink of its flesh. Bruno took the knife again, made a cut in the breast and another two in the front legs, grasped again the flayed hide that was now hanging halfway down its back and tugged it hard. You need some strength to tear hide from flesh, but he used more force than was necessary, putting into it the anger that he had kept bottled up ever since I had arrived. The skin came off in one piece, like a dress. Then he grabbed hold of one of the horns with his left hand, fumbled with his knife between the vertebrae of its neck, and I heard the crack of fractured bone. The head came off with the hide and Bruno stretched it on the ground, with the fur lying on the grass and the skin facing upwards.

The chamois looked much smaller now. Skinned and decapitated, it no longer even looked like a chamois—just meat, bones, cartilage—like one of those refrigerated carcasses hanging in cold storage in supermarkets. Bruno inserted his hands into the thorax and tore out the heart and lungs, then turned the carcass around. He felt with his fingers to find the veins of the muscles along the backbone, severed them with a light cut, and then went back over the line he had followed, plunging the knife in. The flesh that was disclosed then was of a dark red color. He cut off two long cords, dark and bloody. His arms were daubed with blood now too. I'd had enough, and did not stay to witness the rest of the butchery. I just saw at the end the skeleton of the chamois hanging from the branch of the tree, reduced to next to nothing.

A few hours later I told him that I was leaving. At the table I had tried to resume our conversation from the day before, this time being more direct. I asked him what he intended to do about Anita, what arrangements he had made with Lara, and whether he intended to visit them at Christmas.

"Probably not at Christmas," he answered.

"So when?"

"I don't know, maybe in the spring."

"Or *maybe* in the summer, right?"

"Listen, what difference does it make? It's better that she stays with her mother, isn't it? Or do you want me to bring her up here, to live this kind of life with me?"

He said *here* just as he'd always done, as if at the bottom of his valley there was an invisible border, a wall erected only for him, preventing access to the rest of the world.

"Perhaps you should go down," I said. "Maybe you're the one who needs to change your way of life."

"Me?" said Bruno. "But Berio, don't you remember who I am?"

Yes, I remembered. He was the cowherd, the bricklayer, the man of the mountains, and above all he was his father's son: just like him he would disappear from the life of his child, and that was it. I looked at the plate in front of me. Bruno had prepared a hunter's delicacy, the heart and lungs of the chamois cooked with wine and onions, but I had barely touched it.

"You're not eating?" he asked, disappointed.

"It's too strong for me," I replied.

I pushed the plate away and added: "Today I'm going down. I've got a few work-related things to sort out. Perhaps I'll come back to say goodbye before leaving."

"Yes, of course," said Bruno, without looking at me. He didn't believe it and neither did I. He took my plate, opened the door, and threw its contents outside for the crows and foxes, creatures with less delicate stomachs than mine.

• • •

In December I decided to go and visit Lara. I made my way up the valley as the snow was beginning to fall, at the start of the ski season. The landscape was not so very different from that of Grana, and while driving it occurred to me that to a certain extent all mountains look the same, except that here there was nothing to remind me of myself or of someone I once loved, and that made all the difference. The way in which a place can be a custodian of your history. How you could read it there every time you went back. There could only be one mountain of this kind in anyone's lifetime, and in comparison with that one all the others were merely minor peaks, even if they happened to be in the Himalayas.

There was a small ski resort at the head of the valley. Two or three businesses in all, of the kind that were struggling to survive, what with the economic crisis and climate change. Lara worked there in a restaurant built in the style of an Alpine lodge, near to where the ski lifts began and as fake in its way as the artificial snow on the pistes. She came forward to embrace me wearing the apron of a waitress, and with a smile that could not conceal how tired she was. She was young, Lara; she was no more than thirty—but for a good while now she had been living the life of an older woman, and it showed. There were few skiers about, so she asked one of her colleagues to cover for her and came to sit at a table with me.

While talking she showed me a photo of Anita: a blond, rather frail, smiling child who was hugging a black dog much bigger than herself. She told me that she was in her first year of school. It was difficult to convince her to conform to certain rules; when she started she was like some kind of feral child: she would get in a fight with someone, or would begin to scream, or would sit in a corner the whole day saying nothing. Now, little by little, perhaps she was becoming civilized. Lara laughed. She said: "But the thing she likes most is when I take her to some farm. There she feels at home. She lets the calves lick her hands—you know, with that rough tongue of theirs—and she isn't afraid at all. And it's the same with goats and with horses. She's happy with every kind of animal. I hope that won't change, and that she'll never forget it."

She stopped to sip some of her tea. I saw that her fingers around the cup were red, her nails bitten down to the quick. She looked around the restaurant and said: "You know I also worked here when I was sixteen. All winter, Saturdays and Sundays while my friends went skiing. How I hated them."

"It's not such a bad place," I said.

"Oh yes it is. I never thought I'd come back here. But as they say: sometimes you have to take a step backwards in order to move forwards. That is if you have the humility to admit it to yourself."

Now she was referring to Bruno. As soon as we got onto the subject she came down hard on him. She told me that two or three years previously, when it was clear that the farm was not viable, they still would have been able to find solutions. Sell the cows, rent out the farmstead, both look for jobs. Bruno would have been quickly taken on at a building site or dairy processing unit, or even on the ski slopes. She could have worked as a shop assistant or waitress. She was ready to make this choice, to lead a more ordinary life until the situation improved. Bruno, on the other hand, did not want to know about it. In his mind there was no possibility of alternative lives. And at a certain point she realized that neither she nor Anita, nor what she had believed they were building up there together, were as important as his precious mountain, whatever that really meant to him. The moment she realized this, the relationship was over for her. From the very next day she had begun to imagine a future far away from there, with her little girl but without him.

She said: "Sometimes love exhausts itself gradually, and sometimes it comes to an end suddenly: isn't that how it goes?"

"Well, I don't know anything about love," I replied.

"Oh right, I'd forgotten."

"I went to see him. He's up at Barma now. He wants to stay there; he's not coming down."

"I know," said Lara. "The last of the mountain men."

"I don't know how to help him."

"Forget it. You can't help someone who doesn't want to be helped. Leave him there where he wants to be."

Saying this she glanced at her watch, exchanged a look with her colleague at the counter, and got up to go back to work. Lara the waitress. I remembered when she used to guard the cows beneath the rain, proud, still, with her black umbrella.

"Say hello to Anita for me," I said.

"Come and see her before she's twenty," she said, and then she embraced me a little more tightly than before. There was something in that embrace that her words had not communicated. Emotional turmoil perhaps, or nostalgia. I left as the first skiers were arriving for lunch, with their helmets and their all-in-one suits and their plastic boots, looking like aliens.

• • •

The snow began falling suddenly and heavily at the end of December. On Christmas Day it snowed even in Milan. After lunch I was looking out of the window onto the avenue of my childhood, with a few cars passing gingerly along it and one skidding at the traffic lights and coming to a halt in the middle of the crossing. There were children throwing snowballs. Egyptian children who had perhaps never seen snow before. In four days' time I would be catching the plane that would take me back to Kathmandu, but I wasn't thinking about Nepal now, I was thinking about Bruno. It felt like I was the only one who knew that he was up there.

My mother came to be next to me at the window. She had invited her friends to lunch, and they were chatting tipsily at the table, waiting for dessert. There was a joyful atmosphere in the house. There was the nativity scene that she set up every year with the moss she collected at Grana, the red tablecloth, wine, and good company. I envied once more her talent for friendship. She had no intention of growing old sad and alone.

She said: "In my opinion you should try again."

"I know," I replied. "But I don't know if it will make any difference."

I opened the window and stretched my hand outside. I waited for a snowflake to land on my hand: it was heavy and wet and melted instantly on contact with my skin—but I wondered what it would be like now at two thousand meters.

So the next day I bought snow chains on the motorway and a pair of snowshoes in the first shop in the valley, and joined the queues of cars that were going up from Milan and Turin. Almost all of them had skis on their roof racks: after recent seasons without much snow the skiers were rushing to the mountains as if to the reopening of an amusement park. Not one of them took the turning at the junction for Grana. After just a few bends I stopped seeing anyone else. Then, when the road curved past the rock, I entered into my old world again.

There was snow piled up against the stables and the log-built haylofts. Snow on the tractors, on the tin roofs of shacks, on the wheelbarrows and piles of manure; snow that filled the ruined buildings and almost completely concealed them. In the village someone had cleared a narrow strip of road between the houses, perhaps the two men I saw on a roof throwing down the snow that had accumulated up there. They looked up without deigning to acknowledge me. I left the car a little further on, where the snowplow had been stopped or perhaps just given up, having cleared just enough space to turn around and head back. I put on gloves, since recently my fingers tended to freeze in the slightest cold. I fixed the snowshoes to my boots, climbed over the wall of hard snow that blocked the road, and went into the fresh snow beyond it.

It took me more than four hours to cover the route that in summer would take fewer than two. Even with the snowshoes I was sinking almost knee-deep. I was finding my way only by remembering it, gauging the direction from the contours of bumps and slopes, from a still discernible passage between the snow-clad pines, without any track to follow, or any of my usual points of reference on the ground. The snow had buried the remains of the cable lift's winding gear, the ruined walls, the piles of stones quarried from the pastures, the stumps of centuries-old larch. All that remained of the river was a hollow between the two gently sloping humps of its banks: I crossed it at a randomly chosen point with a leap into fresh snow, falling forwards onto my hands without injury. On the other side the incline became increasingly steep, and every three or four steps I would slip back, taking a small avalanche with me. Then I would have to use my hands as well, pointing the snowshoes as if they were crampons and trying again with more determination. Only on reaching Bruno's farmstead did I fully realize just how much snow had fallen: it had reached halfway up the windows of the stable. But the gusts of wind had swept the side facing the mountain, forming a tunnel a footstep wide, and I stopped there to get my breath back. The grass in that small strip of ground was dead and dry, gray as the stone walls. There was no light—and no other color but white, gray, and black. And the snow was continuing to fall.

When I arrived at the top I discovered that the lake had disappeared along with everything else. It was only a snow-filled basin, a gentle depression at the mountain's foot. And so, for the first time in many years, instead of going around it I headed straight across in the direction of Barma. It seemed most strange, walking over so much water. I was halfway across when I heard someone calling.

"Oh!" I heard. "Berio!"

I raised my eyes and saw Bruno much higher up the slope, a small figure above the treeline. He waved, and as soon as I waved back he threw himself down. Then I realized he must be wearing skis. He was coming down at an oblique angle, with his legs opened wide and without any style, just as he did when coming down the snowfields in the summer. He also held his arms open and his chest thrust forward, keeping a precarious balance. But in front of the first larch trees I saw him throw himself to one side and steer decisively, avoiding the wood by crossing higher up, down to the main gorge of the Grenon, where he stopped. In the summer a small stream flowed in that gorge, but now it was a broad snow-filled slide that reached, unobstructed, all the way down to the lake. Bruno assessed the steepness of the incline over the distance remaining between us, then pointed his skis in my direction and set off again. In the gorge he immediately picked up speed. I don't know what would have happened if he had fallen there, but he kept upright, swooped into the basin and gradually braked on the flat, sliding to where I was and coming to a standstill.

He was sweaty and smiling. "Did you see that?" he said, breathing heavily. He lifted one of the skis that must have been thirty or forty years old and looked like some kind of military relic. He said: "I went down to get a shovel and found these in my uncle's cellar. They've been there for years; I don't know who they belonged to."

"But when did you learn how to use them?"

"About a week ago. Do you know what's hardest? Not looking at a tree if you think you're about to collide with it. If you look, you're sure to hit it—bull's-eye."

"You're crazy," I said. Bruno laughed and clapped me on the back. He had a long gray beard, and his eyes were lit with euphoria. He must have lost some weight, as his features were sharper than ever.

"Oh, Merry Christmas," he said, and then: "Come, come on," as if we had met there by chance and needed to go and toast this fortunate coincidence. He picked up the skis and, carrying them on his back, cleared a path for me on the slope along a route that he must have known from his experiments as a skier.

I almost felt compassion for our little house on the rock face, when I saw it surrounded by walls of snow almost as high as itself. Bruno had cleared the roof, and dug a trench around the house which he'd widened into a small square in front of the door. When I went inside it felt like entering into a burrow. It seemed welcoming, and more cluttered and messier than before. The window was blind now; there was nothing to look out at but layers of white on the other side of the glass—and I had barely had time to take off my wet clothes and sit myself down at the table before something fell onto the tiles of the roof with a tremendous thud. I instinctively looked up, afraid that it was about to collapse on me.

Bruno burst out laughing. He said: "Did you fix the rotten ones properly that time? Now we'll see whether the roof holds, eh?"

The thuds continued, but he took no notice of them. When I too had got more used to them I began to notice the changes that had been made to the room. Bruno had put up some more shelves by placing them on nails hammered into the walls, and had filled them with his books, clothes, and tools, giving to the place the air of something that it had never had before—that of a lived-in house.

He poured two glasses of wine. He said to me: "I've got to apologize. I'm sorry things went as they did last time. I'm glad that you've come back, I'd given up hope. We're still friends, right?"

"Of course," I said.

While I started to relax he rekindled the fire in the stove. He went outside with the bucket and brought it back filled with snow, then put it to melt to make the polenta with. He asked me if I felt like having a bit of meat for supper, and I told him that after that slog I would be happy to eat anything—so he took out pieces of chamois that he had cured in salt and put them in a pan with butter and wine. When the water in the pail reached boiling point he threw in a few handfuls of cornmeal. He took out another liter of red to keep us company while we waited, and after the first couple of glasses, as the room filled with the pungent smell of game, I began to feel good again too.

Bruno said: "I was angry. And what made me even angrier was that I had no one else to blame. The fact is that I made all the mistakes myself. Nobody led me into them. What was I thinking, trying to become a businessman? Someone like me who knows nothing about money. I should have fixed up a little place like this one, brought four cows up here, and lived like this from the start."

I kept quiet, listening to him. I understood that he had thought long and hard, and had found the answers he had been looking for. He said, "You have to do what life has taught you to do. Perhaps when you're still very young you can choose, maybe, to change the course of your life. But at a certain point you have to stop and say to yourself: fine, this is what I'm capable of doing and this is what I can't do. This is what I asked myself. And the answer? I know how to live in the mountains. Put me up here by myself and I can cope. That's something, don't you think? But it took me until I was forty years old to realize the value of it."

I was exhausted and was settling down into the warmth of the wine, and even though I would not have admitted it I liked hearing him speak like this. There was something absolute about Bruno that had always fascinated me. A certain integrity and purity that I had admired in him ever since we were boys. I was almost persuaded to believe him, up there in the little house that we had built together: that the best way of living his life was that one, alone in the middle of winter with nothing but a little food, left to his own devices and his own thoughts—even though it would have seemed inhuman for anyone else.

It was the mountain itself that woke me from this fantasy. I heard a sound that was different from the usual thudding on the roof. It began like the roar of an airplane, or like distant thunder—but then got immediately closer, deafening, a rumbling that shook the glasses on the table. We looked at each other, and I could see at that moment that he was no more prepared for this than I was, and no less terrified. To the rumbling another sound was added, that of a crash, something colliding and exploding, and immediately after it the sounds diminished in intensity. Then we began to realize that the avalanche could not have passed over us. It had passed nearby, but elsewhere. More material fell; we felt another, weaker fall, then the silence returned just as suddenly as it had been broken. When everything had stopped moving we went out to try to see what had happened, but by now it was night; there was no moon, and there was nothing to see but the dark. When we went back indoors Bruno did not feel like talking anymore, and neither did I. We went to bed, but an hour later I heard him get up, throw wood into the stove, and pour himself a drink.

Emerging from the burrow in the morning we found ourselves in the light that follows prolonged snowfall. Behind us the sun was shining and the mountain in front of us dazzled the basin. We immediately saw what had happened: the main gorge of the Grenon, the one that Bruno had skied down just hours before, had discharged an avalanche that had started three or four hundred meters further up, at the steepest point of the slope. On plunging down, the snow had dug deep into the ground, so much so as to strip the rock beneath and drag the earth and gravel down with it. The gorge looked like a dark wound now. Crashing into the basin after falling for five hundred meters, the avalanche had gathered enough force to smash through the frozen surface of the lake. That must have been the second sound that we heard. Now at the base of the gorge there was nothing left of the lake's soft expanse, just a mass of dirty snow and blocks of ice, like a serac. The mountain crows were circling above and alighting within it. I could not work out what was attracting them there. It was a terrible and fascinating sight, and we did not need to say anything before going to take a closer look.

The carrion that the crows were sharing was the corpses of dead fish. Small silver trout caught in the midst of their winter hibernation, flung out of the dense dark water in which they slept, up onto a bed of snow. Who knows whether they had time to be aware of what was happening. It must have been like a bomb exploding: from the upturned and shattered slabs I could see that the ice must have been half a meter thick on the surface of the lake. Underneath, the water had already begun to freeze over again. This was only a thin layer as yet, dark but transparent, like the one I had seen in autumn. Some crows were squabbling over a trout nearby, and finding it at that moment an insufferable spectacle of greed I scattered them with a couple of steps and a kick. All that was left behind on the snow was a pink mush.

"Sky burial," said Bruno.

"Have you seen anything like this before?" I asked.

"No, I certainly haven't," he replied. He seemed impressed.

I heard the sound of a helicopter approaching. There was not a cloud in the sky that morning. With the first warmth from the sun, clumps of snow began to fall from every overhang of Grenon, and from the guttering small avalanches fell. It was as if the mountain were starting to free itself from that prolonged snowfall. The helicopter flew above without noticing us and passed on, and then it occurred to me that we were barely a few kilometers from the ski slopes on Monte Rosa, on December 27, on a morning of sunshine and fresh snow. It was a perfect day for skiing. Perhaps they were watching the traffic from up there. I imagined from above the lines of cars, the overflowing car parks, the establishments working to full capacity without a break—and just there, over a nearby ridge, on the side that was in shadow, two men standing at the foot of a landslide surrounded by dead fish.

"I'm going," I said, for the second time in just a few weeks. Twice I had tried, and twice I had failed to rescue him.

"Yes, it seems like the right thing to do," said Bruno.

"You should come down with me."

"Again?"

I looked at him. Something had occurred to him that caused him to smile. He said: "How long have we been friends?"

"I think that next year it will be thirty years."

"And haven't you been trying to get me down from here for the last thirty years?" Then he added: "You mustn't worry about me. This mountain has never done me any harm."

I remember little else about that morning. I was shaken, and too sad to think clearly. I remember that I could not wait to leave the lake and the avalanche behind me—but that later on, once I was down in the valley, I began to enjoy the descent. I found the route by which I'd come up, and discovered that with the snowshoes I could go down in great leaps even at the steepest points, as the fresh snow did not give way beneath my feet. The steeper the incline, in fact, the more I could launch myself and let myself go. I stopped only once, when crossing the river, because I had thought of something and wanted to see if it was true. I climbed down between its snow-covered banks and dug in the snow with my gloves. Just below it I found the ice, a thin transparent layer that broke easily. I discovered that this thin crust protected a vein of water. You could not see it or hear it from the path, but my river was still there, coursing beneath the snow.

• • •

It turned out that in the winter of 2014 the Western Alps had the heaviest snow for half a century. In the highest ski resorts they recorded three meters of snow at the end of December, six at the end of January, eight by the end of February. Reading these figures in Nepal I could hardly begin to imagine what eight meters of snow would look like in the high mountains. It was enough to bury the woods. So much more than was needed to bury a house.

One day in March Lara wrote to me asking me to phone her as soon as possible. She then told me that Bruno could not be found. His cousins had gone up to check on him, but at Barma nobody had been clearing the snow for some time: the little house had disappeared beneath it, and even the rock face was barely visible. The cousins had called for help, and a rescue team taken up by helicopter had dug down to the roof. They had made a hole in the tiles, and at that point had expected to find him—as sometimes happened with the old mountain folk—having taken to his bed with a sudden illness and died there of hypothermia. But there was no one in the house. Nor could any tracks be found in the surrounding area after the recent snowfalls. Lara asked me if I had any ideas, since I had been the last one to see him, and I said that they should check if there was still a pair of skis in the storeroom. No, they were not there either.

The mountain rescue team began to search the area with dogs, so for a week I called every day, hoping for news, but there was too much snow on the Grenon, and with spring the worst period for avalanches arrived. In March the Alps suffered many: and after the events of that winter, in which the death toll on the Italian mountainsides had reached twenty-two, nobody took much interest in a local man lost from view in a deep valley above his own home. It hardly seemed necessary to Lara or to me to keep insisting that they should prolong the search. They would find Bruno with the first thaw. He would turn up in some gorge in the middle of the summer, and the crows would be the first to find him.

"Do you think that this is what he wanted?" Lara asked me over the phone.

"No, I don't think so," I lied.

"You managed to understand him, didn't you? You understood each other."

"I hope we did."

"Because it sometimes seems to me that I never knew him."

And then I asked myself who was it that had known him on this earth except me? And if what was between us was kept secret, that which we had shared, what was left now that one of us was no longer there?

When those days came to an end, and the city became unbearable, I decided to take a tour in the mountains on my own. Spring is a wonderful season in the Himalayas: the green of the rice paddies dominates the sides of the valleys; a little above them the rhododendrons are in flower. But I didn't want to go back to a familiar place, or to retrace the path of any memory—so I chose a region where I had never been before, bought a map, and set off. I had not felt the joys of freedom and discovery for a long time now. I found myself leaving the trail, climbing up a hillside to reach a ridge, just out of curiosity, to see what was on the other side, lingering in a village without having planned to, spending a whole afternoon amidst the pools of a river. That was our way of being in the mountains, Bruno's and mine. I thought that would be a way of preserving our secret in the years to come. It also came to mind that there was a house up there at Barma with a hole in its roof, and that it would not survive like that for very long. And I thought this as if from very far off.

From my father I had learnt, long after I had stopped following him along the paths, that in certain lives there are mountains to which we may never return. That in lives like his and mine you cannot go back to the mountain that is in the center of all the rest, and at the beginning of your own story. And that wandering around the eight mountains is all that remains for those who, like us, on the first and highest have lost a friend.

ABOUT THE AUTHOR

Paolo Cognetti was born in 1978 in Milan. He divides his time between the city and his cabin six thousand feet up in the Italian Alps. *The Eight Mountains* has spent more than a year on the Italian bestseller lists and has been published in thirty-eight countries. The novel has won both Italy's Premio Strega and the French Prix Médicis étranger.

• • •

Simon Carnell is a poet, writer, and translator. Erica Segre is a writer, translator, and fellow of Trinity College, Cambridge. Together they have translated the bestselling works of Carlo Rovelli, as well as fiction and poetry. They live in a village in the Fens in England with their two children, and travel between Cambridge, Italy, and Mexico, heading to where mountain landscapes prevail.